Rosie's
Last
Adventure

Also by Ann Carroll

ANN CARROLL

Rosie's
Last
Adventure

POOLBEG

This novel is entirely a work of fiction. The names, characters and incidents portrayed in it are the work of the author's imagination. Any resemblance to actual persons, living or dead, events or localities is entirely coincidental.

Published 2007
by Poolbeg Press Ltd
123 Grange Hill, Baldoyle
Dublin 13, Ireland
E-mail: poolbeg@poolbeg.com
www.poolbeg.com

1 3 5 7 9 10 8 6 4 2

A catalogue record for this book is available from the British Library.

ISBN 978-1-84223-291-0

Typeset by Patricia Hope in Goudy 11.2/15.3

Printed by
Litografia Rosés, S.A., Spain

About the Author

Ann Carroll lives in Dublin and taught English for many years in Killinarden Community School. She is married with two grown-up children. This is her sixth 'Rosie' book published by Poolbeg. She has also written *Amazing Grace* and *Laura Delaney's Deadliest Day*.

Chapter 1

Rosie was stunned by the painting: a teenage girl, dressed in a short duffle coat, thick stockings and white boots, was standing outside one of the large houses on a city street. It was a late winter's afternoon. Snow covered the ground, rested on the windowsills and whitened the high roofs. The sky wasn't yet dark but already the streetlamps were pale amber. The girl was leaning forward as if about to step out from the frame. Behind her, in a line, were five others, each dressed in the clothes of a different age, each fainter than the one in front, the last barely suggested, almost fading into the twilight.

Rosie stared, fascinated. Beside her, the Art teacher murmured, "Wasn't I right? Don't those girls look exactly like you? Each of them could be your twin, even that Victorian child with her maid's hat and long dress. She's fainter than the others, but anyone can see she's your double. And look at the title!"

They peered at the lettering which was half hidden by the bottom of the frame and the teacher read aloud:

Rosie and the Ghosts of Other Years, St Catherine's School, Eccles Street, Dec 16th 1963

The girl said nothing. Ms Henry glanced at her, curious to note her reaction. The teacher had seen the picture over a week ago when she'd first visited the National Gallery's exhibition, "Fifty Years of Children's Art". She had wanted to preview the ten best pictures and prepare a talk on each one before bringing the second-years of Collins Community School for a visit.

But this particular scene riveted her. It made her uneasy to see someone so like her student in a streetscape painted decades ago, and she'd returned a number of times during the week to be certain there was no mistake.

Each visit had left her more unsettled and if that was how the picture affected her, then how would Rosie feel if she saw it with her classmates?

Every one of them would be clamouring to show it to her. Every one of them would have a comment to make. It wouldn't do at all. Rosie would have no time to get over the shock, which was why Ms Henry had decided to bring the girl on her own to the gallery first. She'd also decided to say nothing beforehand. Words could not do justice to the picture. The girl would have to see it for herself.

Of course Rosie McGrath was so exasperating anyone would think her teacher had invited her on a trip to purgatory.

"Go with you to the gallery?" she'd said, bewildered. "Only the two of us? During lunch-hour? But why, Miss? What did I do wrong? Is it because I haven't got my project done? And I know I was a bit late into class last week –

2

well, maybe more than a bit late – but honestly, Miss, I'd prefer detention, not that I want to do detention, but –"

Ms Henry interrupted. "Your project, that's it! You'll have to work hard on that and an extra visit to the National Gallery won't do it any harm at all." She wouldn't listen to arguments and a bewildered Rosie had accepted her fate, sorry now she'd ever opted for Art. She'd only picked the subject because she thought there'd be no homework. Certainly if someone had told her she'd be hauled off to look at paintings during her precious lunch-time she'd have chosen Home Economics instead, even though her cooking and sewing were worse than her artwork.

She consoled herself with the thought that at least she wasn't going on the class trip to Cork. Imagine spending a whole week so close to Christmas far away doing an art course! It would mean missing the school disco and losing any chance of making an impression on Hugo Smith in fifth year. Hugo was *so* cool, not silly like some of the boys her own age. Really, she'd rather be bald than miss that disco. But Ms Henry had been very sniffy: "You need all the help you can get with Art, Rosie, and you'd learn a lot from the week in Cork. Your priorities are highly dubious, but it's your decision."

Ms Henry was just too old to appreciate the magic of Hugo Smith. Better to keep her sweet and trot off to this exhibition with her, though in Rosie's view it wasn't fair. A lot of her classmates were behind with their projects and not one of them had been forced to give up a lunch-time.

When they'd reached the gallery, with increasing

excitement Ms Henry had pushed her way through the great doors and, seizing Rosie's elbow, had almost run her through the rooms until they reached the last one in the exhibition. She'd steered her into an alcove, pointed at a painting and said, "It's extraordinary! Those six girls are the image of you, Rosie. I want you to see for yourself."

Rosie struggled to understand. The painting *was* extraordinary. Five of the figures wore clothes she recognised: the school uniform from 1956, the prissy 1943 dress, the ancient jacket of 1920, the smock from 1900 and the maid's outfit from Oak Park in 1870. She had worn these clothes on her visits to the past and each girl in the picture was her. But how could that be? No one had ever painted her portrait, she'd never seen that duffle coat or those ridiculous white boots and she'd *never* travelled to 1963. Yet, looking closely, she could see something that dismayed her. On the first girl's wrist was a watch identical to her own, with its black strap, digital screen and calculator.

Did such a watch exist in 1963?

Swallowing hard she pointed to the first figure, "That can't be me! I wasn't there."

Ms Henry sighed. The shock had been too much. "No, of course it's not you, dear." She saw the girl's pallor and tried humour, "After all, that would make you the oldest schoolgirl on the planet – you'd be nearly my age."

Rosie didn't smile. She couldn't take in what she was seeing. The painting gave her a feeling of dread, as if time were playing tricks, making her doubt who she was, as though she'd somehow lost her memory and missed a vital piece of her life.

She was looking so shocked Ms Henry was beginning to regret the visit. "Perhaps," she said hopefully, "the subject is a relative of yours. Could she be an aunt, do you suppose? Maybe she has forgotten she ever posed for this painting. The artist was very accomplished, don't you think? After all, she was only a schoolgirl herself at the time. What's your opinion?" Ms Henry wanted some reply. It wasn't natural for the talkative Rosie to be silent for this long!

"I have an Aunt Rose. I'm supposed to be very like her." Rosie didn't add that by 1963 Aunt Rose had left school and was in America. She couldn't bear any discussion about the strangeness of the scene. What am I doing there? her mind screamed. Since there was no answer there was no point trying to tease it out with Ms Henry. Better to let her teacher think that there was a reasonable explanation for the resemblance.

"Ah. That'll be her then." Still, the likeness was uncanny and the teacher couldn't shake off her unease. And there was something very strange about the watch the first girl was wearing but she wasn't going to mention that. Rosie was pale enough already.

"I think now that you've seen the picture, you'd be better off not coming on the class visit. You can stay in the library and work on your project."

Rosie was hardly listening. "Who is the artist?" she asked.

The teacher pointed. "Look carefully at that corner of the sky where you can see a drifting blackness, like the beginnings of night. It's actually the result of a signature."

Rosie looked:

Jennie O'Neill

She stepped back immediately, but Ms Henry was looking at her watch and didn't notice her amazement. "I'm afraid we'll have to be getting back to school. I'll give you the exhibition-catalogue and you can read it later."

Eager for fresh air and normality Rosie took the catalogue and stuffed it into her schoolbag, barely thanking the teacher. The lunch-hour traffic and the busy streets couldn't dispel the heavy stillness of the gallery and, back in school, the afternoon classes were no distraction. She couldn't get the painting out of her mind and was so absent and so unlike her usual self the French teacher suggested she go before the last bell.

"You're looking very pale – *ton visage est très pâle, chérie*. Get out before the mob, Rosie. Otherwise you're likely to get run over in the crazy dash for freedom."

"And that's only the teachers!" David Murray piped up. He was Rosie's friend and usually made her laugh, but this time there was no reaction.

"You look kind of shocked," her other friend, Helena, whispered. "Did you get bad news?"

Rosie stared at her, distracted, then picked up her bag and left without a word.

At home she was so lost in thought and so off-colour that Mum said she couldn't be well and must go to bed, growing even more worried when her daughter obeyed without argument.

Rosie put the catalogue away in her bedside locker.

Later, another day, soon, sometime, maybe, she'd look at it. Not now, though. Now she wanted the picture out of her mind.

But that night the artist's signature drifted through Rosie's dreams just as it had on the canvas, trailing across the corner of the sky, barely visible against the growing darkness.

Chapter 2

In the days that followed Rosie went to school as usual. She skipped the class-visit to the gallery and later nodded vaguely when her friends mentioned the picture. And since logically the girl in the painting couldn't actually *be* Rosie, the subject became a five-minute wonder, soon forgotten – except by her. The picture brought back all those journeys she'd made to the past.

She *never* wanted to time-travel again. Five times she'd gone back to another year and much of it had been a great adventure. Sometimes her visits involved taking huge risks, even putting her life in peril. Although she'd been terrified, the danger had also been exciting and nothing in her present life could match it.

She'd been eleven on her first journey, too young to realise there was a heavy price to pay for her adventures. Now, at thirteen and a half, she knew better.

At first she'd thought it was wonderful to meet relatives who were long gone before she was born. She'd loved spending time with Grandad O'Brien. She'd loved meeting her Great-great-uncle Joseph O'Neill as a boy of fourteen, and later she'd had one of her best adventures with his twin sons, Henry and Edward. The person she'd liked most of all though, was Patrick O'Neill, Edward's son. He'd been so brave and daring and between them, back in 1943, they'd foiled a murderous plot and brought the criminal to justice.

But the problem was she'd connected with all those relatives and especially with Patrick. She'd become really fond of them, maybe because they were family. When she'd returned to her own time she'd missed them and knowing they'd passed away long ago didn't help. Coming back to the present meant leaving part of herself in the past. It was a kind of death and she didn't want that experience again.

Rosie thought about Patrick. Remembering the lively adventurous thirteen-year-old of 1943, it was hard to imagine him as an old man. He'd be in his mid-seventies now, if he were alive.

But he couldn't be alive, could he? Rosie mused. Otherwise he'd have contacted her by now and he'd be coming to Gran's Christmas party this year, as he'd promised. She had told him where she'd be living and he'd vowed to get in touch. She could still hear his voice and his exact words.

"If I'm alive, no matter where I am, I'll contact you. I'll be there, Rosie, I promise!"

But it was now December and there'd been no word from him and Rosie had no idea where he was. Once she'd visited his childhood home in Griffith Avenue but no one there had heard of the O'Neills.

She'd gone to great trouble to persuade Mum to have a Christmas party for Gran.

"But she's an old lady, Rosie! In her nineties, for God's sake!" Mum definitely thought this wasn't one of her daughter's best ideas.

"But that's the point," argued Rosie. "You should give her a party while she can still enjoy it!"

"No. The point is: one of your parties would kill her. In fact all that thumping music you love would kill me and your father, never mind your gran."

Rosie had persisted, "You wouldn't have that music." She drew on her time-travels, "You'd have waltzes and such. Old songs like 'Kevin Barry' and 'Hang Out Your Washing on The Siegfried Line' and 'There'll be Bluebirds Over the White Cliffs of Dover'. Minuets and things. 'Lightly Lift your Dainty Dancing Shoe' . . ." Seeing her mum's open mouth, she came to a halt, shrugging. "She'd like that kind of thing."

Mum had been silent as she considered the repertoire. Rosie thought she was going to reject the whole idea. But then she'd swallowed and said, "Yes, well, as long as there are no electric guitars or mad drums. Maybe you're right, the kind of music Gran likes would be nice. A few friends and all the family there. A sing-song!" She smiled at her daughter, then added quickly, "When I say sing-song, I mean for those who can sing."

Rosie swallowed her indignation at the barely veiled insult. If she couldn't sing it wasn't for want of trying and she was fed up at people's reaction to her efforts. But now was not the time to get distracted. "It'd be great to have everyone there," she said. "Aunt Rose and Uncle Henry, Shane and Hattie, Uncle Jack and his family . . ." And Patrick and his family, she added silently. What a nice surprise it would be for Gran to meet Patrick! She was always going on about the different branches of her family and wondering what had become of them.

Now, thinking of Patrick, Rosie couldn't stop the painting coming into her mind. The six figures of herself – five of them dressed in exactly the clothes she'd worn during her visits to the past – they were amazing! But what on earth was she doing in a duffle coat and those awful boots? How had the picture come about? And who was the artist, Jennie O'Neill, whose surname was the same as Patrick's? The questions crowded Rosie's mind and she could not get rid of them. The catalogue was the only place that might have the answers. She would have to look at it.

A moment later she was riffling through the pages until she came to a tiny copy of the picture and underneath, the note:

This fine painting was done by Jennie O'Neill when she was thirteen. The subject is a school friend and the scene cleverly catches the influence of the past on the present, showing the progress of six generations. The unusual watch the first girl wears evokes the future, as do her eyes which look beyond the frame.

The painting was overall winner of The National Art Competition for Schools, 1963.

Shortly after it was completed, Jennie O'Neill was expelled from St Catherine's School, Eccles Street, for reasons unknown. As far as can be established, she produced no further work.

Jennie was the daughter of the wealthy Patrick O'Neill. She was no doubt aware of her family's progress from rags to riches over the generations and perhaps their story influenced this painting.

For Rosie the blurb raised even more questions: What had happened to the family business? Every Patrick O'Neill in the phone book had been a false trail. And why had Jennie been expelled? What on earth had she done? And why had she never painted again? Where was she now? She tried all the Jennie O'Neills in the directory, then the Jennifers, then all the Js but none of them was her. Maybe she had married and now used her married name. Maybe she was ex-directory.

Two things for sure: Jennie was Patrick's daughter and the only link Rosie had to either of them was the catalogue.

If she followed the trail to Jennie she would surely discover Patrick . . .

Rosie sighed. There was no help for it. There was only one way to find Patrick and to answer all questions. She would have to go back to 1963.

Chapter 3

Rosie's other visits to the past had each taken a week, no more, no less. She'd never tried to stay longer or shorter and she'd no idea why a week was enough, it just was. Always when her quest was finished, she'd been pulled in different ways: anxious to come home, afraid that otherwise she'd be stuck there forever and would never see her family again, and at the same time sad and sorry because she was leaving people behind.

Finding an excuse for her absence from home wasn't so difficult this time. "I've changed my mind about Ms Henry's Art trip," she told her parents.

"But you hate Art," Mum said.

"You never stop complaining about it," Dad told her. "And your marks are always rotten. But then your marks in other subjects are hardly –"

"Ms Henry says this course will be a great help!" Rosie interrupted before he brought up any other rotten marks. "Ms Henry says Indigo Jones is a wonderful artist. We're so lucky he is deigning to give us some master-classes, she says."

"*Indigo* Jones?" Dad muttered. "Extraordinary!"

"It's not his real name. Ms Henry says dark blue is his favourite colour and it has shaped his work. She says he's a genius and could inspire a cabbage."

"A cabbage, maybe," Mum said dryly, "But you? You were adamant nothing would drag you off on this trip! In fact if I remember, you said, and I'm quoting your exact words here, 'only a lunatic would want to go'. "

Privately Mrs McGrath thought the teacher was the lunatic and had a lot to answer for. It was a mad time to run an Art course, but apparently the 9th to the 16th of the last month of the year was the only week Indigo Jones was available for the second-years of Collins Community School and Ms Henry wasn't going to deny them an opportunity to work with a master.

"Helena's going. And David Murray. But then their parents want them to learn. Their parents don't make it difficult! You're always telling me I should have more respect for learning and here I am, showing respect, but am I encouraged? No – "

"Okay, okay, no more. You can go," Mum said. "Give me that form and I'll sign it. If you'd said straight off your friends were going we'd have understood your change of mind. How much will it cost us?"

"Er . . . it's free. Something to do with left-over money in the school fund." Her parents were pleasantly surprised. There was in fact a fee, but Rosie drew the line at taking their money. She was feeling dishonest enough already. Another complication of time-travel was all the lies needed to make everything seem normal.

"And don't be ringing me when I'm away," she added. "It's *so* not cool!" And there's no point anyway, she thought.

"Of course we'll ring you," Mum said. "We'll have to know you're safe!"

"You are *so* embarrassing! I'll be the only one getting calls from my parents and in front of my friends. God, that is naff!" She was laying it on but if Mum rang her mobile and got no answer she'd cause havoc.

There was a hurt silence.

"I can text you every night," Rosie said finally. "That way you'll know I'm all right."

After some argument they agreed.

"I hope we don't have to wait till you're twenty-five before you'll talk to us in front of your friends!" Dad grumbled. "It's not such a strange practice, you know. I'm sure there must be some teenagers who think it's normal enough."

"Well, I don't know any," Rosie said, her mind already on the next problem. How *was* she going to text home? She could ask David Murray to do it for her and he'd agree immediately. One of her two best mates, David was great fun and he'd agree to any madcap scheme. But he might also send very weird messages such as: *Ms Henry brings us swimming at midnight* or *There is no food available and we haven't eaten for three days*.

She'd have to ask Helena. Helena was sensible.

"You want *me* to text *your* mum and dad?" Helena was incredulous. "Why? Where will you be?"

"I can't tell you," Rosie said, wishing Helena was a bit more like David. "It's just that I won't get a signal where I'm going. I don't want them worrying and kicking up a fuss and if you just text that I'm all right —"

"What about the fuss they'll kick up if they find out?" her sensible friend said. "I'll be dead! And anyway they'll see it's a strange number so they'll know it's not you!"

Rosie was her most patient self. "I was coming to that. Just pretend to be me, text that my mobile isn't working and that's why I'm using yours. Simple!"

Her friend was frowning, deeply disapproving. She shook her head and sighed, "These are serious lies you want me to tell!"

Helena had recently become a very responsible person and briefly Rosie considered murdering her. Instead she pleaded, "It's in a really good cause. And you won't actually be lying. I will be all right. I promise." This was a hope, not a certainty and she hurried on, "You're the one person I can trust, Helena. No one in the whole world could do this for me except you. It's a huge favour and I'll never forget it. You're my best friend and I can't ask anyone else."

Flattered, the best friend relented. "I'll do it only if you tell me later what you've been up to. Oh, and you have to bring me a present from wherever you've been."

Rosie agreed immediately. Time enough to worry afterwards about those two conditions.

From her previous trips Rosie knew the clothes she was wearing would change the instant she stepped into the past, but everything else she brought would stay the same.

16

There was no point packing clothes since none of them would suit the fashions of the time. And bringing present-day money was no good either. In Rosie's experience the most useful thing was food. She could honestly say a lot of the meals she'd eaten in times past had been horrible. She'd never forget the pig's heart, the tripe, the banana-flavoured parsnips or the semolina, all of which had been passed off as nourishing and delicious when "revolting" didn't begin to describe them!

So, the day before her trip, with the spending money Dad gave her for the week, she bought nibbles and dips, six varieties of crisps, chocolate Kimberley, praline flake-bars, marshmallow-chocs, monster fruit chews and a giant popcorn pack. When these were packed into her rucksack she had space in the long side pockets for the cans of coke. On a whim, she got all her make-up – far more than Mum allowed – and put that in. Then she packed the Art set she'd bought as a gift for Jennie in the large back pocket.

The rucksack was jammed now and Rosie sat beside it on her bed, wondering if she'd thought of everything. Idly she glanced around her. Catching sight of her mobile on the bedside locker, she hesitated. Was there any point in bringing it? There was no way she could phone home across a distance of years, but maybe she could play the games if she got bored.

Stuffing it in with the charger she closed the rucksack. Now she was ready.

Chapter 4

Saturday was bright but freezing. At nine o'clock in the morning the moon had left a white ghost in the sky, as if it had hurried away to find somewhere warmer. The wind cut through the air like a chill blade. Frost laced the railings and whitened the edges of grass and hedges.

In the kitchen Dad tucked into his Saturday fry while Rosie, her breakfast finished, heaved the rucksack onto her back. Mum offered to drive her to the community school, where a bus was to pick up the class. "No thanks. The bag's not that heavy and I'll be there in no time."

Mum didn't protest. She was in her dressing-gown, sitting close to the kitchen stove, nursing a mug of coffee, glad not to have to go out.

At the large kitchen table Gran looked up from her paper, "I hope you've a successful journey, Rosie. I hope you find what you're looking for and sort out all the problems."

Startled, Rosie tried to study her face, but the old lady was once more peering at the newspaper. Surely Gran didn't know what she was up to? She frowned with apprehension and looked at her parents but they passed no comment.

Mum saw her to the door. "What your gran says isn't always clear these days," she told her. "She gets mixed up and vague sometimes. It's only to be expected at her age, so don't take it to heart, Rosie. Her health is good and you needn't worry."

The girl brightened. Perhaps it *was* vagueness.

Rosie set off, not for her school, but for the main road and the bus stop, pulling her fleece scarf up around her face to stop her teeth chattering, and clapping her gloved hands to make them warmer. The tips of her toes began to freeze through her runners and for a second she wished she was wearing the warm sensible boots Mum had bought her, even though they made her look like the Yeti, but then if she were wearing them and she bumped into someone, especially someone like Hugo Smith, she'd have to die on the spot.

Rosie was relieved when the bus arrived and she could thaw out in its warmth. She wiped the condensation from the window and gazed out. Christmas was everywhere. Some of the houses in Drumcondra were festooned with fairy lights and most of the garden trees were strung with delicate white bulbs. Here and there a Santa peered down a chimney, or a bright reindeer and sleigh rested on the top of a roof. The shops near the Tolka River blazed with the season's cheer. The Bishop's Palace on the hill was hidden behind high walls and trees like a palace in an old story. In Dorset Street most of the apartment lights were still on and Christmas trees brightened the windows.

Rosie got off at the end of Eccles Street and, suddenly

afraid of the next step, she went into a nearby shop. The Chinese girl at the till was serving an Asian man while two people behind him chatted away in what Rosie thought might be Polish. She bought a silver torch out of her last tenner, pocketing the change which would pay for the bus journey home, all going well.

Then there was nothing for it but to move on.

Rosie's notion of Eccles Street came from the painting – she'd never actually been there. She reckoned the school was roughly halfway up the street, but when she got to the general area she stopped, amazed.

A large section of the Georgian houses had been demolished and replaced by a modern building and a car park. Bewildered, she stared around her. Where on earth had the school been? She needed an exact location otherwise she might not get back to 1963; worse still, she could end up in God knows what century. Time played tricks on people and if she were wrong by even a couple of feet her journey could be jeopardised.

But how could she find the right place? There was no way of telling where St Catherine's once stood. Faced with the thought of going home, Rosie closed her eyes and groaned.

"Are you looking for the entrance to the hospital, love?" A middle-aged woman was standing beside her.

"No, no. I'm just wondering where St Catherine's used to be." God, if she had to go home, how was she going to explain the fact that she wasn't on her way to Cork? Her parents would insist on contacting Ms Henry with whatever excuse Rosie gave and then . . .

And then didn't bear thinking about.

"St Catherine's School? Janey, that's gone ages ago, long before you were born. You're a good many years too late, love, if you want to enrol there!" She laughed, adding, "If I may say so, you're way behind the times, love."

This was no help at all and mentally Rosie rolled her eyes, wondering what she should do next.

"I remember the place well myself," the woman said. "I used to be a maid there, cleaning and polishing and serving the food and when I left I got a lovely reference from Reverend Mother Misericordia."

"Are we standing where the school was?" Rosie held her breath.

"No, love. See over there, to your left, the granite rock in the corner behind the railings? That roughly marks the spot where the front door was. The friends of St Catherine's got together to buy it. The school name is inscribed on it. And do you know why it was put there, love? Because generations of girls passed through St Catherine's and it's not right that the school should disappear as if it never existed. Mother Misericordia would weep if she knew."

They both looked hard at the granite, thinking about the past but each in a very different way.

After a moment the woman said, "Sorry, love, you probably find all this boring."

"No, I don't," Rosie said. "I think it's really interesting."

Encouraged, the woman smiled, "Nearly all the girls there were friendly, very good-hearted. Really nice to me they were. They always called me 'Ellen', and I was supposed to call them 'Miss', but most of them wouldn't

21

have it. Mother Misericordia was lovely, on her good days that is, but she wasn't exactly calm. She had a desperate temper. Like a bomb ready to explode, so she was. Old Misery was her nickname and –"

"Do you remember any of the girls?" Rosie asked, having no interest in this litany.

"It was all a long time ago, love. I remember very few. There was one who was always painting, gifted she was, Jennie somebody, I think."

"Jennie O'Neill," Rosie murmured.

"That's it. My goodness, you're right."

"She's a relative," Rosie explained.

"Well, isn't that a wonder! Full of personality she was. Poor girl, she got into terrible trouble over some party. That was the rumour anyway. I don't know exactly what happened because no one talked about it. But it must have been a shockin' scandal because suddenly she wasn't in the school any more. I think she was expelled and I remember Mother Misericordia at the time was entirely frazzled."

"Is Jennie the only one you remember?"

"No, now I think of it. There was another girl called Stacia Bolger. Actually, I've never forgotten *her* name, though I've tried. Fancied herself goodoh. Thought she was too high and mighty to talk to the likes of me, except to give orders or be nasty. She didn't like Jennie O'Neill. There was great rivalry between them. Stacia Bolger was older and a prefect and she just loved making trouble." The woman stopped, still pondering the past for a few moments, then shook her head, "No point reliving such nastiness. Listen love, I'd best be going. Be sure to give my regards to Jennie O'Neill when you see her. Mention Ellen and she might remember me." With that the woman went on up the street, turning once to wave and smile.

When she was gone from view, Rosie looked around. For the moment, Eccles Street was empty.

Swiftly she changed the date on her watch to 9.12.1963. Then she took the catalogue from her bag and found the painting. Closing her eyes, she concentrated. She had no idea what Jennie looked like and so she thought of the six figures, of the Georgian buildings and of St Catherine's all those years ago.

The hum of distant traffic died away and the atmosphere stilled. The wind was silent. There was no sound. It was as though she were profoundly deaf. Then Rosie sensed an indefinable change and heard a long sigh as the air breathed once more. Snow began to fall and sounds, faint at first, separated into voices, the noise of an engine, a bicycle bell, nearby footsteps.

Rosie opened her eyes.

Metres away from her girls were filing out of two old-fashioned single-decker buses, dragging cases with them.

"Why do we have to spend a week in St Catherine's?" one girl was loudly protesting. "Why couldn't they just send us home early for Christmas?"

"Because they like to make us suffer!" her companion said. Then her voice changed, imitating authority, "'Lifelong learning is our motto in this school and will not be interfered with by a little diphtheria. Lolling about at home serves no useful purpose. St Catherine's will have you translating Caesar's *Gallic Wars* before you come back to us.'"

"That's very good, Olivia. You sound exactly like Old Betsy!"

They shrieked with laughter.

"You girls! Yes, you two. Are you referring to Mother Elisabeth?" A very angry nun in a long cream habit, her face a red triangle in a starched wimple and collar, steamed up to them. "Such disrespect!" she fumed. "I would remind you that as principal of Aquinas College, Mother Elisabeth deserves deference. Old Betsy, indeed! You make her sound like an ancient jalopy."

"Sorry, Mother. We didn't mean her to sound like an ancient jalopy," the girl called Olivia said, hanging her head.

The other got a fit of giggles which she turned into a cough.

The nun wasn't fooled. "Stop sniggering at once. Your attitude is deplorable and does not bode well, not well at all."

The two girls tried to look crestfallen. "Awful sorry, Mother," they said.

"My name is Mother Misericordia." The nun drew herself up. "Please use it when you address me. You will be here for at least a week and if nothing else St Catherine's will put manners on you. Now, hurry up!"

She ushered them up the steps and Rosie saw the two girls grin at each other before they disappeared through the door.

She studied the altered street: the old houses with their

fanlights, a parked black Anglia and a tiny cream Fiat 500, a youngish woman putting on a headscarf against the falling snow – coat and skirt very short, a youngish man pulling up his collar, a cigarette at the side of his mouth. His overcoat had huge buttons on the shoulders and down the sleeves.

"Stop dithering, girl!" Mother Misericordia beckoned from the doorway. "No hanging around in the streets for you girls. It's a rough, common practice and we're all ladies here." She eyed Rosie a little sourly. "Most of us, that is."

Confused, Rosie said, "Are you expecting me?"

The nun glared at her, "We have no time for comedians or smart alecs. If Aquinas College hadn't come down with diphtheria, St Catherine's wouldn't have to put up with the likes of you and that other pair. You'd better watch yourself, my girl!"

On her way up the steps, Rosie tripped and the catalogue fell through a gap in the railings and into the basement. For a moment it lay on the concrete, pages flapping, then, in the blink of an eye, it vanished.

"Quickly, girl. Don't dawdle."

Rosie stepped over the threshold and into St Catherine's.

Chapter 5

She took in the long dark wide hall, the dark wooden floors and the sepia-brown walls. Two ancient lamps of yellowing glass hung from the high ceiling and at the end of the hall she could see a staircase disappearing into the gloom.

"Stacia Bolger!" the nun called and an older girl in a hideous uniform emerged from the darkness of the stairwell. All uniforms were horrible in Rosie's opinion but this was worse than most: the wine pinafore had a cross-over top and a skirt with about two thousand pleats which made the girl look huge. The neat cream blouse underneath and the wine cardigan, with the sleeves rolled up, reminded Rosie of a picture she'd once seen of a washerwoman at a tub of dirty laundry. All that was missing was a kerchief tied around the girl's head and knotted at the top.

Silently Stacia Bolger came up the hall, unsmiling and unfriendly.

Mother Misericordia was checking her list. "What's your name?" she said to Rosie.

"Rosie. Rosie McGrath."

The nun peered at the page. "Oh for heaven's sake!" she spluttered. "I don't know who made out this list in Aquinas, but the names are either misspelt, wrong altogether, or missing." She glared at Rosie, "You're one of the missing. A bit of illness and the whole system goes wrong." She shook her head and sighed loudly. "It can't be helped. What year are you?"

"Second year."

"Second year, *Mother Misericordia,* if you please! I was told Aquinas was sending all second years to our Waterford college. Another example of poor management. 2A will have to make a space for you." She turned to the older girl. "Stacia, take this child to the second-year dormitory. She'll have the extra bed in the alcove. Make sure she deposits that outlandish bag and then bring her to class."

"Class? Class?" Rosie could not help her astonishment.

"Yes. Of course. You have heard of class? Lessons? Teachers and so on? Desks, blackboard, chalk, books, copies. These are familiar to you?"

Not on a Saturday morning, Rosie wanted to say. Class on a Saturday was barbaric. But since Mother Misericordia was peppering with sarcasm she kept these thoughts to herself and followed the older girl up the staircase to the fourth-floor dormitory.

Two rows of narrow iron beds, a dozen altogether, made a perfect straight line on either side of the huge room. Beside each was a large locker and the distance between the beds was exact. A couple of enormous wardrobes flanked either side of the door like giant sentries standing

27

to attention. The polished wooden floor creaked at every step. Dark green velvet curtains hung on the long sash window at the far end of the room and bottle-green walls completed the gloom.

"You're over there." Stacia Bolger smiled as she pointed to a corner in the shadows.

Rosie saw the outlines of a bed and locker.

As she put her rucksack under the bed, Stacia told her conversationally, "A girl died in this dorm about ten years ago. Caroline Browne was her name. She came here in second year, just like you. No one liked her and she hated the school. Such a baby. She wanted to go home, but her parents were abroad for the year. One term was all she spent here. In her last few weeks she couldn't sleep and used to walk the corridors at night."

Stacia paused, and in the silent shadows her pale face and lank hair gave her a sickly, almost spectral look. In spite of herself Rosie was impatient to hear the rest.

"One mid-December night there was a terrible snowstorm. Next morning Caroline wasn't in her bed. And she didn't come to chapel or appear in the refectory for breakfast. They began to look for her and finally, someone went out to the garden. It was freezing. Icicles hung from the trees, the frost crackled and it hurt to breathe because it was so cold. If Caroline had been there she would have been a frozen statue. She wasn't, but the searcher looked up and saw a deathly figure at a high window in the storeroom on the corridor outside this dorm. It was Caroline. No one ever found out why she went there. When they got to her she was shivering and whiter than the snow. The poor girl had pneumonia.

She died in that bed – your bed – just after midnight." Again Stacia paused and the shadows seemed to grow darker.

Rosie was about to ask how anyone could know this was the deathbed, but Stacia anticipated her.

"Her initials are carved on the side of the bedstead. Have a look. You'll need the light." Stacia crossed to the door and switched on the ceiling lamp. The orange glow cast more shadows and made the room even gloomier, but when Stacia held up the mattress and bedclothes Rosie could make out the letters CB on the metal.

"Someone did that after she died, so that there'd be no mistaking whose bed it was. No one would sleep in it, even though the head nun of the time said it was a shocking waste. After Caroline's death, the bed was put in the storeroom. It might have stayed there till kingdom come except for this emergency. Once, a few years ago, a girl was dared to spend the night in that bed, in the storeroom, but she lasted less than an hour and would never speak about the experience afterwards." Stacia paused to let the words hang, then lowered her voice to a whisper. "They say Caroline Browne cursed the school before she died. And they say she still walks the corridors up here."

Rosie blinked, pulling herself together. There was something too slick about this story, as if Stacia had learned the words off by heart and had used them many times before. Still, she had to give the girl credit: she was a class A storyteller. But that stage whisper at the end – it was so exaggerated. It was her way of frightening newcomers but no one from the present could be fooled by all that guff. Ghosts belonged to fairy tales.

Rosie yawned. "Yeah, right. If St Catherine's has a ghost, then I'm from another century." The words were careless and her mind shouted, *'You are from another century!'* She hurried on, "I suppose her ghost appears every night."

Stacia's eyes narrowed. "Not every night, no, only near Christmas, around the time of her death. Caroline vowed that one day the school would be destroyed and not a brick would be left. She promised to come back every December until then."

Rosie was shaken. The other girl could not know what would happen to St Catherine's and though Rosie didn't believe in ghosts, nevertheless the words were eerie.

Stacia saw her unease. "I thought it was only fair to warn you. Then if you see her it won't be such a shock." With her calculating look, the girl was like a fox waiting for a mesmerised rabbit to move.

Rosie shrugged. "Thanks, but you needn't have bothered. Only fools believe in ghosts."

Stacia reddened. "Are you calling me a fool?" When she got no answer her mouth tightened, but all she said was, "We'll see who's stupid. For now you'd better follow me."

She clattered down the stairs and through a warren of passages, so fast it seemed to Rosie she was trying to lose her, which made her determined to keep up.

Finally Stacia waved at a door, "Your class. 2A." She strode on, pausing briefly to call back, "A is for Asses like you." The words were silly but the venom in Stacia's voice shocked her. It was obvious to Rosie she had made an enemy.

30

Chapter 6

Rosie tapped on the door.

Inside a woman's voice was chanting: "*Dominus, domine, dominum, domini, domino, domino. Domini, domini, dominos, dominorum, dominis, dominis.* Lord, oh lordy, girls! We did all this before. You should have it off by heart like the Lord's Prayer. All together, now: *Dominus, domine, dominum . . .*" The class joined in the chorus.

Rosie had never heard the like before. When the chant finished she took a deep breath and knocked hard.

"*Veni!*" said the woman. Rosie knocked again and this time the door was pulled open. "*Veni nunc, puella!*" A young woman wearing a professor's cloak and dressed in a very short black skirt, ribbed white polo-neck and thigh-length boots was frowning at her. Rosie stared, mesmerised by the boots and the gown.

"Why didn't you come in when I told you? Who are you?"

"Rosie McGrath. From – er – Aquinas College. Mother Misericordia sent me to 2A."

Inside the murmur died away.

The frown turned to a smile. "Ah. You must be feeling a little lost. *Veni et benevenitas*. You know your Latin, I hope? Have you no books? Why didn't you leave your coat in the dormitory? Never mind. You're allowed to be scatty on your first day. I'm Miss Minahan and I'll get one of the girls to look after you. I don't suppose you know anyone in St Catherine's?"

"I know Jennie O'Neill. Well . . . not exactly know . . ."

But the teacher had already turned and Rosie followed her into the class. There were three rows of old-fashioned desks, most of which had two occupants and they were all silently staring at Rosie. Their uniforms again made her think of buxom washerwomen.

For the first time she noticed her own clothes: the brown duffle coat, the white, tight, shiny boots and the heavy stockings were a surprise to her, though they shouldn't have been. The stockings were so thick they must be bullet proof, she thought. Unbuttoning the coat, she groaned. She was wearing the same uniform as the others.

"Jennie O'Neill," Miss Minahan was addressing a girl with long shiny copper hair and bright green eyes, sitting at the front of the class, "I want you to look after this girl from Aquinas. You're the only one she knows. Now, Jennie, I've already separated you from Katie MacAllister for talking, so don't pass on your bad habits to the new girl."

The girl looked bewildered, "I've no idea who –" she began, then broke off, catching Rosie's pleading eye. "All right, Miss. I'll look after her."

Rosie put her coat on the back of the chair and sat down, relieved.

"Coming from Aquinas College, I'm sure you know your Latin cases off by heart, Rosie." Miss Minahan smiled at her.

Rosie looked vague and hoped for the best.

"We will go through the noun *Dominus* again. Singular and plural, give me the nominative, vocative, objective, genitive, dative, ablative. Ready?"

Rosie had no idea what Miss Minahan was talking about. She didn't want to know either. None of it sounded pleasant, but Miss Minahan nodded encouragingly at her as the class started the chant: *Dominus, domine, dominum* . . .

Slowly the teacher's expression changed to puzzlement as Rosie stayed silent. She leaned forward, studying her, and said, "Once again, class."

This time Rosie reckoned she'd have to say something. She barely opened her mouth and hoped the teacher couldn't lip-read.

"*Eeny meenee minee mo,*" she said, "*erno domino, atchy batchy toory-atchy, um, dum, dutch.*"

Miss Minahan smiled, satisfied, but Jennie O'Neill was overcome by a fit of the giggles. Just as the teacher was about to quiz her, the bell rang, and Miss Minahan set their homework: a translation from English into Latin from *Longman's Latin Primer*.

That should be great fun, Rosie thought.

Miss Minahan came over. "You're not related, are you?" she asked.

"No, Miss." Jennie said. "We don't even look alike."

But in ways they seemed very alike, the teacher thought

as she left. They had different colouring but their smiles were similar, and their expressions, and they had both tilted their heads to the left, looking quizzically at her in exactly the same way.

"What's next?" Rosie asked.

"English with Locky – Miss Lockhart. And Miss Minahan's called Minnie." Jennie laughed. "Your English can't be worse than your Latin!"

Rosie decided then it would be better if the other girl knew about her trip back to the past. Very soon people would realise she hadn't a clue what was going on and start asking questions. To survive she needed Jennie's help.

For now she said, "I don't know any Latin."

"You must know some."

"I never learned any."

"You must be doing Latin in Quinos."

"I'm not actually in Aquinas College."

"But you told Minnie –"

"I lied."

Jennie's mouth dropped. Who was this girl? Why had she said she knew her? Why had she no books and no Latin? And where did she get the Saint Catherine's uniform? Jennie had seen some of the girls from Quinos at toilet-break half an hour ago and they were wearing their own green uniform. What was going on?

Before she could ask, the English teacher arrived. The class stood and in unison said, "Good morning, Miss Lockhart." They sat down in silence.

"You may open your poetry books, girls. You have five minutes to go over the poem."

Miss Lockhart, formidable in her professsor's cloak, was middle-aged, grey-haired and steely and today was the day she was going to hear each person in the class recite the whole of Gray's "Elegy in a Country Churchyard".

All around girls had their heads down, muttering away. Rosie looked into Jennie's book and saw that the poem was very long. "How many verses?" she whispered. Somehow she knew talking would not go down well with Miss Lockhart.

"Thirty-two."

"Thirty-two!" Rosie squeaked, drawing Miss Lockhart's attention.

Glad of any excuse to distract the teacher, one of the girls behind Rosie put up a hand and said, "There's a new girl in the class, Miss. She's Rosie McGrath and she's from Quinos, Miss – I mean Aquinas College."

"Thank you, Katie MacAllister. You are welcome, Rosie. Please don't come to class again without your books. One warning is sufficient. Now, Katie, please recite the poem."

Katie stood up, managed seven verses and stumbled. Miss Lockhart waved an imperious hand and Katie brought her copy up to the teacher. Glumly she sat down again.

"Punishment exercise," Jennie whispered, "for anyone who doesn't know at least ten verses."

Miss Lockhart went around the entire class but no one could recite the thirty-two stanzas. A few like Jennie managed about twenty. A few more were summoned to the teacher's desk with their copies.

Rosie was so amazed by this carry-on she remained

silent, thanking her good fortune that in Collins Community School no one had to learn off any poetry, never mind thirty-two verses. She looked at the first line: *The curfew tolls the knell of parting day.* What did that mean?

Miss Lockhart wouldn't let anyone rattle the lines off, she wanted them recited clearly and, as Rosie listened, she began to like the peaceful sound and slow rhythm even though she grappled with the meaning.

After the last girl had given up the teacher sighed. "You've been learning the poem during the last three weeks. You managed two verses a night. Why can't you put it all together?"

Since this was a criticism rather than a question, Miss Lockhart didn't expect an answer and was taken aback when Rosie said indignantly, "No one could learn thirty-two verses of anything. It's too many. And the poem makes no sense. It's as bad as Latin."

She heard a suppressed giggle from Jennie and a huge intake of breath from the class.

Miss Lockhart's look was steely, her words cool. "You are a stranger in our midst, Rosie McGrath. How do you know the poem makes no sense to anyone here?"

Rosie went scarlet as she tried to defend herself. "Well, I can't understand one word."

"Really. And have you studied it?" Miss Lockhart's smile was thin as the girl shook her head. "Luckily that's a disadvantage we can remedy. Jennie O'Neill, you were highly amused at your companion's somewhat ignorant outburst. Perhaps you'll still be laughing when you've explained every verse to her. As for you, Miss McGrath, I expect you to know the poem by rote next Friday. Do I make myself clear, both of you?"

Crestfallen they muttered, "Yes, Miss."

"Good. Now, girls, it's a beautiful poem, more than two centuries old. Each stanza is splendid. There is no point in knowing about a poet's life and all about his themes without knowing a word of what he has written. As for learning thirty-two verses, it can be done. Listen."

Miss Lockhart closed her poetry book and recited the poem. In spite of herself Rosie was captured by the sound, even silently repeating a few phrases. Some of the meaning became clearer. Enraptured by the teacher's voice, she imagined herself in that old graveyard at twilight over two hundred years ago.

The lines drew to a close and the silence lingered until Miss Lockhart coughed and briskly said, "Five shillings for the person who best recites the full poem next Friday. We'll leave it aside till then and start Dickens' *A Christmas Carol*. Since the past lacks appeal for you today, your essay for next Tuesday is 'The Future'. You can tackle it any way you like as long as you do three interesting pages. No codswallop."

While the class took note Rosie calculated that five shillings was worth maybe thirty cents and Miss Lockhart's inducement, in modern money, worked out at less than a cent a verse.

The class and Miss Lockhart rose with the bell. Bags were packed and from the chat around her, Rosie realised it was lunch-time and lessons were over till Monday. Life in the classroom wasn't going to be easy.

A few of the girls smiled at her as they left. Katie MacAllister, usually inseparable from her best friend, Jennie, remembered Miss Lockhart still had her copy and rushed after her.

Jennie hung back till the others were gone, then she told Rosie, "We'll have to follow them down to dinner, but you owe me an explanation. You've no Latin, no books and you're not from Quinos. You know who I am but I don't know you. Something very strange is going on. You'll have to tell me, especially if you want me to cover for you."

Chapter 7

Jennie led her to 2A's table in the refectory. Rosie was the centre of attention. They asked her if it was true that sixty girls in Quinos had come down with diphtheria, that some wouldn't get home for Christmas, and some were so ill they might not recover.

"Well . . ." Rosie didn't know what to say. They were all looking at her, frowning with concentration, waiting for an answer.

"How would she know?" Jennie said. "The nuns hardly gave her a bulletin every day, did they? They wouldn't want to be spreading bad news, would they? So they hardly ran up to her and said, 'Glory be to God, Rosie, we want *you* to know the fine detail: there's thirty-one and a half down today!' Can you imagine Old Misery doing something like that here?"

The image startled them into laughter. Then they hushed as someone warned, "Oh no! Here she is."

A sudden silence descended. At the top of the refectory Mother Misericordia stepped onto a platform, closed her eyes and blessed herself. Everyone stood. "Grace Before Meals," she announced, her voice low with a hint of menace. Woe betide anyone who stepped out of line.

Rosie looked around her, fascinated, as, heads bowed, the girls recited the short prayer and then listened to a piece from "daily scripture". This was unlike anything she'd ever come across before.

The reading over, they waited.

"Before you sit I'd like to welcome the girls from Aquinas College. I am Mother Misericordia, Principal and Head of Discipline. No doubt you've already heard of me, but I'm afraid if any of you come to my attention during your stay, it can only mean trouble. As guests of St Catherine's you will of course behave impeccably and acquaint yourselves with our rules. Now you may sit and talk. Food will be served."

Mother Misericordia clapped her hands. Immediately five girls in black dresses, white aprons and maids' caps appeared from behind the platform, each pushing a trolley of food towards a table.

Rosie stared at the smiling waitress who served her. "Ellen!" she said. "You're Ellen."

"Do I know you, Miss?"

"Not yet," Rosie said.

Someone opposite asked Rosie why she was wearing a St Catherine's uniform when all the other Quinos were wearing their own green pinafore.

It was a good question, but she had no idea what the answer was. Every time she'd come back to the past she'd found herself in clothes she'd never have chosen in a thousand years. Whoever decided these things had vile taste. Whoever decided these things had gone mad altogether this time and given her the wrong uniform. But this would hardly do as an answer. The girl opposite was waiting, very interested.

"It's a spare uniform," Jennie once more rescued her. "The nuns always have a few of them. Rosie's the only second-year here, so it's easier if she's dressed the same as the rest of us."

At once Rosie realised this was actually the right reason. It meant everyone from Quinos would think she was a St Catherine's girl, so there'd be no awkward questions unless someone told them otherwise, which wasn't likely to happen if she kept out of their way.

The Powers That Be weren't mad after all.

Rosie ate the Irish stew and rice pudding without relish. Her answers about Quinos were vague though she brought Old Betsy into the conversation whenever anyone mentioned teachers. In the end she decided the only way to get off the topic was to ask plenty of questions herself and so she learned that Mother Misericordia got her nickname 'Old Misery' because she caused so much suffering.

"She's not human," Katie said gloomily. "She gives detention if she catches you breathing. It's true," she added, catching Rosie's smile. "I got two hours for sighing at Mass. I didn't even know I was sighing. She gave me *The Life of Christ* to read. I might think Mass was painful, she said, but *The Life of Christ* would teach me the true meaning of pain. Well, she was right and I haven't sighed since."

Locky, Rosie learned, wasn't as bad as she thought. "She

won't take any cheek," one girl said, "but she's fair. And she's a brilliant teacher."

"Expecting you to learn thirty-two verses of poetry doesn't seem fair," Rosie said.

"Yes. Well, she's mad about poetry and like she says, that poem is great."

The murmurs of agreement surprised Rosie. If people in Collins Community School liked poetry they kept it to themselves. The English teacher, Mr Robeson, had told them, "Remember you don't have to quote verses for your exams. You only have to know the gist of the poem." He hadn't said learning lines was a waste of time, but he hadn't said it wasn't.

2A also liked Minnie. She was great fun, for a Latin teacher. Sometimes she told them about her social life, about the dances she went to, which were proper dances and not just tennis-club hops. Minnie went to the Olympic Ballroom or the Four Pees, places full of romance, with real musicians like Brendan Bowyer and the Royal Showband. The Four Pees didn't sound very romantic to Rosie but she said nothing, aware that people in different times had different views.

Some of the class had met Minnie and her boyfriend one Saturday afternoon and had been introduced to Anton. Anton was a beautiful name. They all sighed, even Katie. They loved the way Minnie dressed, she wasn't one bit square and she liked the Beatles and she was the youngest teacher in the school. The rest were ancient, but she was often mistaken for one of the pupils. One of the day-girls said Minnie was on the same bus home as her at half twelve one day and the conductor only charged her a penny. The teacher was mortified, told him she wasn't a schoolgirl and tried to pay the full fare. "You couldn't be more than fourteen," he said. The day-girl said she and her pals got a terrible fit of laughing which the conductor took personally. He thought Minnie was making a joke of him and threatened to put her off the bus which made them all even more hysterical.

Rosie thought 2A were far too interested in their teachers. They should get out more, she mused, but then as boarders perhaps they hadn't much freedom. At least they'd lost interest in asking her about Quinos.

With 'Grace After Meals' over, Jennie signalled to Katie to wait a moment. "Will you do me a favour?" she asked, once the three of them were on their own.

Katie nodded.

"I'm not coming to hockey. If people ask, especially Stacia Bolger, say I'm around somewhere. Don't tell her I'm staying here. I want to talk to Rosie, show her the school, tell her the rules and all that."

Sport was compulsory on Saturday afternoons. According to Mother Misericordia, dispensation from the Pope himself wouldn't get them out of it. Only those who were sick or dead were reluctantly excused. Mother Misericordia was a grim woman. Luckily even those who hated sport looked forward to the afternoon and willingly walked a mile to the sports field. It was a great chance to meet the boys from St Ivor's.

"What about Alan?" Katie said. "He'll be disappointed you're not there."

43

"He probably won't notice," Jennie said. But if he mentions me, say we'll see him and Brian tomorrow if we can get away from the walk. Tell him to bring a pal for Rosie."

Rosie raised an eyebrow, sure no one could match Hugo Smith and anyway she had no interest in meeting a boy from 1963 – he'd be ancient in her own time. But she smiled and pretended enthusiasm. She pictured Hugo. "I'd like someone tall," she said, "with dark hair and blue eyes, with cool, cool clothes, no spots, and a motorbike . . ."

"Would James Bond do?" Jennie rolled her eyes. "Put in a request, Katie. Make sure to ask for someone who keeps his bell-bottoms in the fridge."

By two thirty the corridors were quiet. Since the girls never mitched from sport, no one was on patrol. Most of the nuns were out visiting or working in their own quarters. Occasionally one or two would appear on their way to the chapel, but they were easily avoided.

The two girls made their way to the dormitory, tip-toeing up the stairs and past the nuns' parlour. The only other person they saw was the young maid, who was dusting the banisters on the top floor. She beamed at them.

"If you see anyone coming up to the dorm, Ellen, will you tell us?" Jennie said.

"I will, Miss."

"Jennie, not Miss. And this is Rosie."

Once they were in the dormitory, Jennie said, "Now tell me what's going on."

"You won't believe me."

Jennie settled on her bed and pointed to the one beside it. She was a good listener and without interruption Rosie told her who she was, where she was from, how she discovered her gift for time-travel, the journeys she'd taken to the past and especially the one to 1943 when she'd met Patrick O'Neill, Jennie's father. She described Patrick's house on Griffith Avenue, the wartime food, the shortages and, in detail, the adventure they'd had.

She told the girl about her own family, how Gran was so old, yet always eager to find out about the different branches of the family. Finally she told her about the Christmas party and Patrick's promise to be there. She had come back to find him, because she'd expected him to get in touch by now and he hadn't and she could find no trace of him in her own time.

The only thing Rosie didn't mention was the painting in the National Gallery. It felt creepy to bring up a picture that Jennie couldn't have even thought of yet.

By the time she'd finished, the room was growing dark and she could not read her companion's expression. The girl said nothing. She doesn't believe one word, Rosie thought. It all sounds so extraordinary. She must think I'm the greatest liar . . .

The silence grew.

At last Jennie shifted and sighed, "It's unbelievable."

"But it's true." In spite of her immense disappointment, Rosie's voice was steady.

"I know," Jennie said. "My father talked about time-travel when I was small. He said he'd met someone when he was thirteen who came from the future – a girl called

45

Rosie. He told me of her adventures and they match the ones you're telling me about now. I never forgot his stories but I thought they were bedtime tales and he was making them up, the way fathers do. But he wasn't, was he?"

"No." Delighted that Jennie believed her, the words tumbled out. "This is brilliant. When can I meet him, remind him about the party? I know he'll want to come and Gran will be so pleased!"

"You can't meet him. He and my mother moved to New York in September. There's some crisis in the American side of the business. They wouldn't take me with them because they want me at school here. It's why I'm a boarder. They've let our house in Dublin for a year."

Rosie's hopes collapsed. It seemed success had been snatched away when it was almost in her grasp.

"When I was small," Jennie mused, "I used to ask him to tell me one of your adventures. I was fascinated by them: murder in the dark, lonely woods; moonlight smugglers out in Howth. But for all that he said, he never mentioned your gran, or a party. And he won't be back here any time soon, Rosie, that's for sure. The company is owed a lot of money in New York and he has to sort that out. If it isn't paid, the business will collapse."

Her journey was a waste of time. Disappointed, Rosie felt trapped. She was stuck for a week in this awful place, with its rice pudding and umpteen rules and prayers, its Latin and its Gray's *Elegy* and its horrible people like Stacia Bolger and cranky Old Misery. And what for? She could put up with it if there were any chance of meeting Patrick, but now it seemed there was no point to it at all.

"Your gran's party . . ." Jennie said slowly, trying to work out the complexities of time. "It's not for more than forty years."

"No. In my time it's in a couple of weeks," Rosie said.

Jennie pondered. "But we're not in your time. My father isn't thinking your party is on this Christmas and he has to get home. Your time is years into the future for him. There's no rush, Rosie. Even if he forgot the promise he made, you can remind him. You can write a letter and I'll give it to him. It's 1963 and he has all the time in the world – well, a few decades anyway."

She was right. Rosie felt a bit stupid. She should have thought of that! After all, *she* was the experienced time-traveller, not Jennie! But then her spirits lifted. She could contact Patrick through his daughter. There was a point to coming back after all.

Yet moments later disappointment came again. Less than a day back and the big problem was solved. She had faced very little risk or danger. If she wasn't supposed to be in Cork now, she could go home. The only good thing about the trip was meeting Jennie, but the thought of having to spend the next six days in St Catherine's was depressing. She'd just be killing time. How would she stand it?

Chapter 8

Ellen was still working, polishing wood and cleaning the odd brass doorknob. By this time she had worked her way down to the ground floor and was daydreaming about the nice tea her mam would have ready when she got home. The fire would be lit and later on she'd watch *Juke Box Jury* and *Wells' Fargo* before going to the local hop with her best pal Julia. She loved Saturday nights.

She never heard Stacia Bolger padding up behind her and jumped with fright when the girl spoke. "Have you seen Jennie O'Neill?"

At once the young maid got more flustered. She didn't want to be caught out in a lie by someone as mean as Stacia Bolger, who'd often pushed her out of the way or barged into her for no reason. "What do you want her for?"

Stacia raised her eyebrows. "I don't have to explain myself to the likes of you."

"Why would I know where Jennie O'Neill is?" the maid said.

Stacia's brows rose higher till it seemed they might

disappear into her hairline. She gripped Ellen's skin just above the elbow, held it between her thumb and forefinger and began to twist. "But you do know where she is, don't you? Now tell me."

The spot on her arm was burning and Ellen felt her skin might be twisted right off. The agony was unbearable. "She's in the dorm with the new girl from Quinos!"

Stacia smiled, gave another twist then climbed the stairs, slowly and nonchalantly. When a lion is after a mouse, she seemed to say, there's no need for hurry.

Ellen on the other hand slipped down a side passage and zoomed up the back stairs as if she were being chased by the same lion. On the fourth floor she rushed along a twisting corridor, through the horrible storeroom and into the gloomy dormitory.

"Stacia Bolger's coming!" she panted, sick with breathlessness.

Galvanised, Jennie stood up. "Does she know I wasn't at hockey?"

"So what if she does?" Rosie was scornful.

Jennie had no time for explanations. "Come on!" She rushed from the room.

"Jesus, Miss! Don't leave me!" the maid gasped and Jennie rushed back, seizing the girl by the arm. "Come on!" she urged.

The three of them had got as far as the storeroom when they heard the footsteps.

"Shhh!" hissed Jennie. "In, and close the door. Don't move."

In the dusty gloom Rosie could see the outlines of a

wardrobe and a chest of drawers and shelves piled with books and papers. Something else caught her eye – a white wavering shape at the window. Perhaps it was a curtain. No one spoke and the silence was broken only by Ellen's laboured breathing. The steps halted outside, the handle turned and the door creaked open.

Rosie found the tension unbearable.

"*Boooooh! Yaaaagh!. Wheeeeeaou!*" she yelled.

The door banged shut and the footsteps pounded away.

Triumphantly Rosie turned to the others. "That got rid of her." But her companions had flown out the other door and already were clattering down the back stairs. She was alone.

Her eyes were drawn now to the shape at the window. It suddenly ballooned, dominating the room. There was a rustle and a sound of harsh breathing. Rosie froze, mesmerised. A long sigh chilled the air. Then a door banged in the distance, breaking her trance. She ran.

They were waiting for her on the back stairs.

"Jesus, Mary and Joseph, Miss, what were you doing, roaring like that?"

"I was trying to frighten Stacia so she wouldn't come into the room."

"You had us terrified," Jennie said. "I thought you'd seen a ghost."

Rosie decided not to mention the white form at the window. It was probably nothing anyway, a curtain, or a sheet over an old sofa, maybe. And it was probably her own breathing she'd heard. No point in making the others even more fearful.

They left Ellen at the bottom of the back staircase just as the five o'clock bell was ringing for tea.

"Let me tell you about Stacia Bolger," Jennie said. "She's one of the five sixth-year prefects. Each of them takes care of a class – 2A, in her case. We're supposed to be able to talk to her, tell her our worries. But we'd sooner ask a boa constrictor for a hug than ask her for advice. She's meant to look after us at hockey, but she hates hockey and always turns up ages after the rest of us. Then she starts shouting and giving orders and looking for an excuse to report us to Old Misery."

"If a prefect is supposed to be caring and sympathetic," Rosie said, "how did she get to be one?"

"Because she's one of Misery's pets, and Misery thinks care and sympathy are bad for you. Anyway, if Stacia finds out I wasn't at hockey she'll report me."

Rosie was disappointed to think Jennie wanted so desperately to stay on the right side of authority.

"If I get into trouble again," Jennie told her, "Misery says I won't be allowed to travel to New York. I'll have to spend the holidays here. In St Catherine's. With the nuns. Can you imagine?"

"No, I can't. But sure she can't keep you here, not against your parents' wishes."

After a moment, Jennie sighed. "That's the trouble. I think they'd find it easier with all the worries they have if I didn't go to New York for Christmas. I mean, they won't say so, but they might be happy to leave me here."

"Patrick wouldn't do that," Rosie said, remembering the boy she'd known.

51

"Not normally he wouldn't," Jennie agreed. "But you don't know the state they were in."

Tea was a boiled egg and plenty of bread and jam and a currant bun. This time there was no nun on the platform. Instead Stacia Bolger was standing there. Solemnly she waited till everyone filed in, then bowed her head, closed her eyes, joined her hands, and with an expression of extreme holiness she led the Grace. Prayer finished, she nodded graciously: "You may sit and eat."

Her expression changed when she looked across at Jennie. Extreme holiness turned to extreme poison. Self-importantly she strode over to 2A's table. Katie just had time to mutter, "I didn't tell her anything, just said you must be around somewhere."

"You weren't at hockey, Jennie O'Neill." The prefect was on the attack.

"Who says?"

"I do. I didn't see you there."

"I didn't see you either. What does that prove?"

"You think you're so clever!" Stacia was sure of her ground and her voice oozed triumph, "But I knew you were up to something so I came back to school early, on my own, and that scut of a maid told me you were in the dorm with your pal here." She flicked a hand at Rosie without looking at her.

"So?" Jennie said. "There was nothing to stop me getting back to school early either. I was a sub today, on the benches, not playing."

"Ah," Stacia was smug, "but no one in 2A is allowed to return without me."

"And you're not allowed to return without 2A, Stacia. You shouldn't have come back on your own." Jennie grinned. If she had broken the rules, so had the sixth year. Mother Misericordia would punish both of them if she found out.

"That's right," Katie added her support. "We looked everywhere for you after the match, Stacia."

Since 2A disliked the prefect, they all added their complaints, grumbling about the ages they'd spent looking for her when all the time she'd gone back without telling them.

Defeated, Stacia flushed with anger and was about to walk away when Jennie added, "I'm sure you'll be interested to know, Stacia, I got an idea this afternoon for the National Art Competition."

For a moment the prefect was speechless. She blinked, opened her mouth a couple of times, then shut it again. When she gathered her wits she shrugged, "I don't know why you think I'm interested. You're full of yourself, you are, if you think you've any chance of winning."

She strode off. The table buzzed with delight. Stacia was a pain and it was about time she got her comeuppance. If Jennie could beat her in the art competition that'd be a victory not just for her but for the whole class.

Glancing up, Rosie was the only one who caught Stacia looking back, her eyes malevolent.

Chapter 9

After tea there was an hour's homework. Realising Rosie could be in deep trouble if she showed up in the Study Hall with no books or copies, Jennie came early and broached Mother Misericordia. "I've lost a lot of my books, Mother, so I can't do much study."

Mother Misericordia drew herself up. "Drivel," she said. "Absolute drivel. I've no time for such nonsense." She lifted the great bunch of keys that hung on a chain from her waist. Swiftly she unhooked one. "Open the lost property room. Find books and come back instantly."

Rosie was waiting outside the hall. Fifteen minutes later they had collected enough tattered dusty books, half-filled copies and chewed pens to do Rosie for the week. Along with an old scissors, she stuffed them into a worn satchel she'd found under a heap of scarves and jumpers.

Mother Misericordia took back the key and waved imperiously towards two empty desks. With a finger to her lips, she motioned strict silence.

As quietly as possible Rosie cut the used pages from her

copybooks. She turned the brown-paper covers inside-out and wrote her name on each one.

Mother Misericordia was absorbed in her own work. From time to time she raised her head but, apart from the odd rustle, nothing disturbed the silence.

Rosie started writing:

> 20, Innish Road,
> Whitehall,
> Dublin.

Dear Patrick,

Today I came back from 2007 to 1963. I was looking for you but could only find Jennie which is why I'm stuck here in St Catherine's. (She will tell you the story.) I'm glad I met her. She is so cool the way she stands up for herself and the way she's helping me.

I thought I'd be able to find you in the 2007 phone book, but you're not listed. I tried a few internet sites too, looking at Irish companies, but yours isn't there. I even tried the web under 'oldfriends.ie' but no luck. It's funny because there are so many ways to get in touch in my time – mobile, fax, landline, email, all that stuff – but in the end I had to come back to the past and write this letter.

Gran is getting very old so I hope you'll come to her Christmas party. Remember your promise? Well, 2007 is the year, so you've still got plenty of time.

Even though she's really ancient, Gran loves doing new

things and is great on the computer. She did a course called, 'Google For Golden Oldies'. Of course you don't know yet about Google, do you? It's cool. If you want to find out about Ancient Rome or American movies or 'I'm a Celebrity, Get me Out of Here', (which is a TV programme about famous people who do things like eating worms or letting ants crawl all over them) all you have to do is ask Google. It's kind of an online encyclopaedia. Lately though Gran is using the computer to find out more about her family and all its different branches, so I know she'd love to see you.

You haven't met Mum and Dad yet but I think you'd like them. Dad is mad into classical music and has about five hundred symphonies on his i-pod. He wears his earphones for hours and is always conducting the orchestra, waving a hand, eyes closed. I'm so glad we're the only ones who see him doing this. Sometimes I shake him but only in an emergency because he jumps sky high and his language is really foul.

He says he's going to wear a big 'Do Not Disturb' sign but if he does I am leaving home because he is too absent-minded and will probably wear it to the cinema or something and if people like Hugo Smith see him I could never speak to them again.

Dad is not a rational person though, because when it's me listening to my i-pod he says he can't understand people who allow such a tiny machine to take over their lives.

I told you Mum is a solicitor. These days she is doing a lot of work for the immigrants. She says it's a disgrace the way they are treated and sometimes they can't even get a bus without being picked on and it's the same on the Luas and the Dart. We should remember our own past, she said, and when I asked her to explain this I was sorry, because she went on and on for hours.

By the way you can ring my mobile phone in 2007, the number is 089325729. It might be on silent if I'm in school, but you can leave a message on the voicemail. Otherwise use the landline.

Gran loves surprises and I know she'll be really happy with the party, especially if you're there. For her last birthday Dad hired a stretch limo for the afternoon. It had a chauffeur and a huge bottle of champagne on ice. Gran was so chuffed. She said I had to have a glass of bubbly too. Mum and Dad were glaring, but after a few drinks they didn't notice what anyone else was having any more. Mum ended up wearing the chauffeur's cap and Dad and Gran took turns singing all these ancient songs by the Beatles and Vera Lynn. But I didn't mind because the limo had dark glass and no one outside could see us and Gran loved it all. She kept saying afterwards what a wonderful surprise it was, but I know you turning up at her party will be even better.

That's all I have to tell you for now except for one more thing. I'm not expecting a reply to this letter, not for a good few years anyway.

Hope you ring in 2007.

Love,

Rosie.

She read over the letter, hoping she hadn't forgotten anything important. Suddenly Mother Misericordia appeared beside her. The large woman with the huge bunch of clanking keys had achieved a miracle and moved so noiselessly no one had noticed in time to warn Rosie.

The copy was snatched from the desk and the nun puffed up with anger. "How dare you," she steamed, "write a letter when you are supposed to be doing homework!"

Jennie turned to listen, startled.

"Who is this Patrick?" continued the nun. "I hope it is not a boy. We in St Catherine's do not encourage communications with boys. We are, I hope, more serious-minded. And what is this rubbish? *Today I came back from 2007 to 1963. I was looking for you . . .*"

By now everyone was listening, knowing too well if Rosie's letter was to a boy, she was in desperate trouble. Mother Misericordia did not like boys. She thought their intentions were dishonourable and sometimes referred to them as Occasions of Sin. No girl should ever go out with one on her own, she said. Having a boyfriend was against school rules, so if this letter was to a boy . . .

Rosie was furious. "You shouldn't read someone's –" Before she could say anything else, Jennie interrupted, her voice shrill.

"Essay! Essay. It's our English essay, Mother. The title is 'The Future'. Rosie's writing as if she's someone from the future sending a letter to someone in the past. She's going to invite them to a party."

Mother Misericordia looked at both girls in turn. Their gaze was innocent. "Well then," she said at last, "you won't mind if I read the rest of it, if it's only an essay?" Without waiting for an answer to what wasn't really a question the nun went back to her seat.

When Study was over Mother Misericordia handed Rosie the copy. "Your essay isn't altogether clear," she said, "and your imagination runs away with you. We will never have stretch limousines in this country. They are an American abomination. Nor will we have immigrants, though I dare say you're right about television. It can only get worse." As an afterthought she added, "By the way, you haven't drunk champagne, have you? That was a little flight of fancy, am I right?"

"Yes, Mother," Rosie said.

The nun was satisfied though afterwards she wondered which question the girl had answered. Afterwards too she wondered about the girl's clothing and concluded that Jennie must have found her an old St Catherine's uniform.

Later they were allowed to see *Bonanza* on Telefís Éireann in the second-year common room. Rosie wondered how anyone could watch black and white TV, especially with the screen slipping and spots everywhere. Grumbling to herself about the reception, she nodded off just as Little Joe galloped out of Il Ponderosa, ready for another adventure.

Then someone played 'The Hucklebuck' on an old turntable. Half-asleep, Rosie wondered was she hearing things: *"Wriggle like a snake, waddle like a duck, that's how you do it, do the huckle buck!"*

Afterwards an exciting mug of cocoa was followed by a decade of the rosary and then it was bedtime.

Wearily Rosie climbed the stairs to the dorm. She had brought no clothes of any kind and was tempted to get into bed in her uniform, so tired was she. First though she must put her rucksack away. Opening the locker she saw enough underwear for the week and a pair of wine plaid pyjamas in thick flannel. God, they're hideous, she thought. But at least they were warm and when she put them on no one made any comment, possibly because everyone's pyjamas were the same. Even the PJs were uniform.

The sheets were freezing, but a bed of ice wouldn't have stopped Rosie sleeping. It had been a long day, she thought, drifting off, and nothing troubled her slumber until morning.

Chapter 10

The noise shattered the peace. It clanged up the stairs and along the corridors, getting louder and louder, till Rosie felt her head would burst. Opening her eyes she sat up.

Stacia Bolger was in the doorway, vigorously swinging a large brass bell. Only when everyone was out of bed, holding their ears and begging her to stop did she move away, still jangling their nerves for a few more minutes. The silence when it came was blessed.

In the bathroom, Rosie noticed the cubicles around the washbasins. "I'd love a shower," she told Jennie.

"Bath night is Saturday. I'd have mentioned it last night but you were too tired."

Making do with a washbasin, Rosie thought the sixties were uncivilised.

Later, as she was putting on her uniform in the dormitory, Jennie said, "Why don't you wear your Sunday clothes?" And she saw the others had on short skirts and ribbed sweaters. One girl wore a V-neck jumper back to front.

"Don't tell me you've only got your uniform? Come over here." Quickly Jennie took her to one of the huge wardrobes and opened it, pointing. "Those are mine. Pick a jumper and skirt, but hurry. We've to be at Mass in ten minutes."

Rosie took a dark kilt and white sweater.

"Here, you'd better borrow these louis heels too," Jennie said, handing her a pair of extremely pointed shoes with dainty heels. "You won't get away with your boots again. I'm surprised Old Misery said nothing yesterday. Indoor shoes are the rule."

She could stab someone with these shoes, Rosie thought, but at least they fit.

They were just in time for Mass. The school chapel was pleasantly gloomy, its stained-glass windows casting blue and orange lights on the dim interior. The polished wooden benches were full. A line of nuns sat at the back and except for the odd cough and shuffle of feet there was silence while they waited for the priest. The Mass was in Latin. The warmth, the priest's quiet voice, the strange language lulled Rosie's senses.

There were more prayers before and after breakfast and a reading from the gospel for the day. Rosie wondered were the nineteen sixties religion-mad but no one else seemed to think all this prayer was strange. Everyone around her blessed themselves rapidly, intoned the words as fast as they could, said "Amen" and immediately talked about something else. As far as Rosie could see no amount of praying interrupted what they were thinking or what they wanted to say.

On Sunday mornings the girls were left to their own devices as long as they stayed indoors. They could use the common room to read or listen to the record player. Some of them wrote letters home. They bought sweets when the school tuck shop opened. But their freedom stopped short of going out. This was against the rules. They couldn't cross the threshold unless accompanied by a prefect. Even then there had to be a very good reason and permission had to be sought from Mother Misericordia.

Jennie badly wanted to go out, but not with Stacia Bolger watching her every move. "You know the National Art Competition I mentioned yesterday, Rosie?" she said after breakfast. "Well, I really do have an idea for it. But I need your help. The picture has to be finished by Friday so I have to work fast, too fast to get anywhere, probably."

They set out to find Mother Misericordia.

Jennie was most polite. "May I leave the school, Mother?" She saw the frown of refusal begin to crease the nun's forehead and hurried on. "It's for the Art competition. I want to paint Rosie at the front of the school."

The nun was about to say it was out of the question, but Jennie pushed further.

"And we don't need a prefect with us, Mother. You'll be able to see us all the time from the nuns' room and, after all, there's no one better than you at watching people, Mother."

Old Misery thought she detected sarcasm, but Jennie's expression was so sincere and flattering she must have been mistaken.

"Please, Mother. I'll have to work hard to get the

picture finished. I might have a chance if I start now on the sketches."

The word "work" swung it. The Head had a great respect for work. It was idleness that led to all the trouble in the world.

"As long as I can see you both," she conceded. "And don't forget your outdoor shoes."

So Rosie found herself spending the morning outside, once more wearing her white pointy-toed boots which, in her opinion, were fit only for a pantomime. There must have been something seriously wrong with people in the sixties, she thought, to put such objects on their feet.

Jennie made various sketches of Rosie: on the steps at the front door; on the path by the railings; under the streetlight with the row of houses in the background. There was Rosie facing the artist and Rosie in profile, there was Rosie sitting on the steps and even Rosie swinging around the lamppost. Just as Rosie was getting sick of it all, Jennie closed the sketchbook and smiled. "Finished," she said.

Mother Misericordia, seated at her window, was most impressed. Not once had Jennie looked up to see if she were there. The girl was so absorbed that there had been no conversation, apart from making requests of the sitter. And as for that child from Aquinas College, well, she wasn't the nincompoop she'd seemed at first, when she'd behaved as if she'd never heard of Saturday classes. Anyone who was willing to spend a couple of hours being bored beyond endurance in order to help someone else rose sharply in Mother Misericordia's estimation.

Too busy to take a detailed interest in every subject, the nun wondered if Jennie O'Neill had any talent. Hard work of course was its own reward, but it would be satisfying if the girl also had a gift, especially since she didn't broadcast it to the world like some people.

She was at the door when the two girls came in and Jennie was quite happy to hand over the sketchbook, thinking the principal was as usual checking up on her.

Mother Misericordia studied each page, her face expressionless. Then she handed the work back. Her praise was faint. "A good effort," the nun said. "You didn't waste your time. Now don't forget to change into your indoor shoes."

Afterwards, Rosie was indignant. "I'd like to see *her* efforts. Bet she couldn't do as well. I don't know how you managed to show how cold it is in pencil. Your sketches are brilliant. I look freezing and the atmosphere is so wintry."

"Which one do you think I should use for the painting?"

Rosie didn't answer and it was Jennie who pointed to the figure under the lamppost with the row of houses behind. "What about that one? Or is there too much space behind you, too much of the path? What do you think?"

Unwilling to make suggestions, Rosie said nothing. No way was she going to reveal that she'd seen the finished painting, because then she'd be tampering with something that needed no interference.

Jennie pondered, "I like the street and the houses and there's something mysterious about you in it. Whatever way you posed, it looks as if you're trying to step out of the picture, as if you don't belong here. I got the watch right.

But there's something missing. All those stories you told me . . ." She gazed intently at the sketch, then looked up, her eyes bright. "All those stories. That's it. You'll have to tell me what you were wearing every time you came back and I can put each figure into the picture."

With that she dragged Rosie off to a dim corner near the refectory and made her relate in detail what she had worn in other times.

Rosie thought the clothes she'd worn on each visit were generally disgusting. They'd been scratchy, stiff and starchy and once even mouldy with age. She could never forget them and gave every detail, expecting sympathy. Jennie tried to hide her increasing amusement, keeping her head down, sketching and taking notes, but as Rosie became more and more disgruntled at the memory of the revolting outfits, Jennie gave a muffled snort, then laughed outright.

Rosie stared at her, astonished, then annoyed. But the girl couldn't stop and was so convulsed Rosie found it catching. The two went into hysterics. At last the fit passed and when Rosie looked at the sketches she was full of admiration. "You've got the clothes just right."

"If it wasn't for you I wouldn't have thought of this painting, Rosie. You've been a great help."

As the bell went and they made their way to lunch, Jennie said mischievously, "By the way, we're meeting three fellows from Ivor's later. Katie says your one is fantastic. Twice as good-looking as James Bond." She choked with laughter again, "He's known as *Double O Fourteen*."

Rosie thought of her white boots and baggy duffle coat. She was sure the fellow would do a runner the minute he saw her. Oh well, his opinion didn't matter, did it? She'd be gone soon. There was no need to feel nervous. He wasn't someone her own age, not really. She just had to remember he'd be ancient in 2007.

Chapter 11

The crocodile wound its way downtown. Two by two the girls dutifully followed their leader, Stacia Bolger.

Rosie was brooding on the unpleasantness of life in the sixties. She'd been led to believe otherwise, especially by her mum. She felt a surge of resentment. Mum was always talking about the freedom she'd had when she was a teenager long ago. "Dublin was much safer then," she'd said. "You could walk anywhere, any time, on your own." She'd forgotten to mention that school had treated people like prisoners. It was ridiculous not being able to go out by themselves.

Every so often Stacia Bolger went down the line to make sure no one was trailing. She was like a warden in charge of a chain gang. How they were going to escape for the afternoon and get away with it was beyond Rosie.

She and Jennie were at the back of the crocodile and Katie MacAllister dawdled with them whenever she could.

"What will happen if we're caught with those boys?" Rosie asked.

"We'll probably be expelled." Jennie didn't sound too concerned.

"That's ridiculous," Rosie said. "You can't be expelled for talking to people."

"Boys aren't people," Katie said. "According to Mother Misericordia boys are A Bad Influence. She says talking to them is the First Step on the Road to Perdition."

"I don't know what perdition is exactly, but Mother Misericordia is mad." About this Rosie was definite.

The others gave the notion serious consideration, then Jennie said, "I don't think she is. She's says we aren't old enough yet to have anything to do with boys. She's a bit old-fashioned, I suppose – square – but not mad. She doesn't want us to get into trouble. Anyway, we're not going to be caught, you'll see."

"I thought this was supposed to be the Swinging Sixties," Rosie grumbled. She had read the phrase somewhere and it had made her think of freedom and fun and a good time. Glumly she thought they should be renamed The Seriously Sad Sixties.

Katie laughed, "Mother Misericordia belongs to the Middle Ages not the Swinging Sixties."

The subject was dropped and they paid keen attention to passers-by as they got closer to town. Katie and Jennie oohed and aahed over a girl wearing a very short rabbit-fur coat and thigh-length boots. A young man caught Rosie's attention. He had dark hair down to his waist, wore platform shoes, bell-bottom jeans and a long green military overcoat that was plastered with ribboned medals.

"What is he like?" Rosie muttered. But her companions

69

were so impressed that Stacia Bolger stormed back and said anyone who whistled again at passers-by would be reported.

The prefect led 2A down O'Connell Street. None of the shops was open but there were plenty of people queuing for the cinemas. Rosie gawped at buskers singing 'She Loves You, Yeah, Yeah, Yeah!'. She gawped at Nelson's Pillar, and she gawped at Clery's window, with a huge collection of 'Famous Dolls' labelled, *Twiggy, Bonnie and Clyde, James Bond, Cilla Black.*

In the middle of them was a nun-doll, 'Sister Sourire,' dressed like Mother Misericordia, only this one was holding a mandolin and wearing a saintly expression. "Who's that?" she asked.

"The Singing Nun," Jennie said. "She was number one on the hit parade."

"What does she sing?"

"'Dominique'. It's about a girl who talks only about God. She was on Top of the Pops, The Singing Nun," said Jennie, confirming Rosie's view beyond any doubt that the sixties were seriously, seriously, sad.

She was distracted by a billboard for the *Sunday Press*.
Jack Ruby in Dallas County Jail for murder of Lee Harvey Oswald.

"I know those names," she muttered. "Jack Ruby . . ."

"He shot Oswald," Jennie said and in response to Rosie's struggling expression, she added, "who killed President Kennedy last month."

"Of course. I remember. And Ruby will die in jail. It's in our History book."

Katie was staring at her. "What did you say?"

Caught out, Rosie turned to Jennie, but the words had shocked her too and she could think of nothing to say.

"There's something strange about you," Katie said slowly. "I mean, you're supposed to be from Quinos, but you don't have the uniform and nobody from that school has even said hello to you. You'd think they'd recognise another boarder."

At last Rosie's wits returned, "All I'm saying is, 'Jack Ruby will lie in jail. One day it'll be in all the History books.' Anyway what do you mean, I'm strange? What are you getting at?"

Katie didn't know what she was getting at. There was something wrong, something very different about Rosie McGrath. It was odd the way she stared at people as if she'd never seen the like of them before. And it was obvious to someone sitting behind her in class that she hadn't a word of Latin. And anyone who wasn't from another planet had heard of The Singing Nun. Rosie must be the most ignorant girl on the face of the earth, but Katie could hardly say so.

"I don't know what I'm getting at," she said. Perhaps she was a bit jealous of Rosie, she thought. The girl seemed to have become Jennie's new best friend, leaving her out in the cold. Katie sighed.

Stacia paraded them across O'Connell Street and up past the GPO towards Parnell Square. At the Carlton cinema huge posters announced:

The Scarlet Blade: Fabulous Feats of Swashbuckling Never Seen Before.

Two young men dressed in tight tartan suits strummed guitars and sang 'Charmaine' to the long queues.

71

So far there'd been no sign of any boys and Rosie was beginning to think they weren't going to turn up. Unexpectedly she felt disappointed. Boys would be interesting. It'd be fun trying to give Stacia Bolger the slip.

She was wondering what the third boy was like, the one Alan Whoever-he-was had been told to bring along for her. Was he tall? Good-looking? She imagined a sixties Hugo Smith. Daydreaming away she didn't notice passing the Gate Theatre, turning the corner and then entering the Municipal Art Gallery. Her thoughts still drifting, when 2A stopped in the hallway she wandered on, oblivious.

Stacia Bolger called sharply: "Hey! Where are you going?" Rosie didn't hear and Stacia's voice rose. "Hey! You! Stop at once! Do you hear me?" Losing patience she roared, *"Are you deaf, Rosie McGrath?"*

Everyone in the entrance hall and the galleries beyond turned around. A uniformed official came over at once, "No hooligans allowed in here," he said. "People come into this gallery for a bit of peace and quiet. If they wanted roarin' and shoutin' they'd be in Croke Park. So you, young one, will have to leave." He took Stacia's elbow.

"But I am in charge here!" Outraged, Stacia didn't lower her voice.

"Stop bellowin', d'you hear me? I've noticed you before with your huffin' and puffin'. You have no respect for others. Out now!"

Stacia was propelled towards the door. She shouted, "2A, follow me at once!" But half-turning, she saw none of them. The class had disappeared.

"Now, you, young one, you listen. If you come back in I'll have to get the gardai. Off with you! Go on, skedaddle!" With that the official brushed his arms and left her outside.

There was nothing Stacia could do but wait.

Chapter 12

The class scattered in various directions as soon as they realised what was happening. They were free until they chose to leave and it was an opportunity not to be missed.

Rosie followed Katie and Jennie as they flew up the stairs and into a small chamber at the back. Three boys were trick-acting their way around the room, paying no attention to the paintings, interested only in pushing and wrestling. There was no one else about.

"Hi, Alan." Jennie suddenly became shy, as a dark-haired boy grinned at her while holding off one of his friends who was trying to trip him.

The third boy turned around and said, "Hi, Katie. Did you get rid of Stacia Crustacia?"

"Can you believe it, Brian, the porter threw her out for disturbing the peace! He threatened her with the police."

There was a moment of solemn silence. The boys stopped shoving each other. Then Brian whistled appreciatively. Alan did a jig. The other boy exchanged looks with Rosie.

He had been brought along for her and they examined each other covertly.

She did not know what to think. His coat was a wild sheepskin down to his ankles and the white wool lining was doing its best to escape, curling up around his neck, reaching down to the floor and out through buttonholes in long tendrils. Perhaps it had once belonged to a huge prehistoric sheep. Rosie could concentrate on nothing else.

"Love your Afghan, Jimmy. It's fab," Jennie said. "Rosie, this is Jimmy Sullivan. Jimmy, this is Rosie McGrath."

The boy smiled at her. His face was nice, she noted, though his fair hair was a bit strange, brushed forward and long at the sides. His jeans were okay, but the shimmering purple shirt he was wearing might give her a headache if she looked at it too long.

"See you at five o'clock at the front door, Rosie," Jennie said. She and Alan were holding hands as they left the room. A moment later the other two followed. Jimmy and Rosie were on their own.

"Dig your boots," Jimmy said.

"What?"

"Your boots. Fab." He wasn't kidding.

"Thanks."

Silence. Rosie coughed. Jimmy dug his hands into his pockets.

"Where did you get your coat?" Rosie said. "I've never seen anything like it, not even in the Natural History Museum."

Jimmy was a little startled, but took it as a compliment.

75

"My cousin got it from someone who brought it home from Afghanistan. Fab, isn't it? Bit smelly though. Don't think the skin was cured properly."

Rosie sniffed. He was right. It ponged and she wrinkled her nose.

Delighted, he laughed. "After the rain it really stinks."

For him the smell was one of its major attractions. When Rosie said there weren't many coats that could produce such an aroma, he knew she was a person of fine judgement. These days "polish" was one of Jimmy's favourite words and he divided people into those who had polish and those who had none. Rosie had polish and he told her so.

"And you're a person of capernosity and function," she replied. They had just read 'The Confirmation Suit' in CCS and it was one of the phrases she liked. Her English teacher said it meant anything you wanted it to mean and she liked that too.

Jimmy beamed and asked did she want to go for a walk. This must have been some kind of code because when Rosie nodded, he immediately gripped both of her hands, leaned forwards and kissed her.

Astonished, her wits scattered and she stood there, paralysed, the passive recipient of Jimmy's kiss.

"Excuse me, you two. You're supposed to be looking at the pictures, not upsetting the clientele." It was the porter from downstairs.

Jimmy stepped back, abashed.

"What clientele?" Rosie said. "We're the only ones here."

"The clientele that might come into this room any

minute and won't want to be distracted by your shenanigans. Right?"

Rosie was about to argue the point but Jimmy, who didn't want to be thrown out into the cold, cut in, "Okay. We're just going down to the caff."

"Well, make sure you do now. I'll be watching the two of you."

In the gallery café, they sat over two hot chocolates and Jimmy chatted. He talked about football (Man United), music (the Mersey Beat, Rock and Roll), his family (two younger brothers) and his love of clothes. As soon as he left school, he said, he'd be heading for London. He'd be finished with lousy pocket money and earn decent wages and spend it in the record shops and the boutiques on King's Road where the clothes were fab. That's where he'd got his shirt, well, where his cousin got it. It was a hand-me-down. But the point was, such a psychedelic shirt could only be bought in London.

At this, he took off the coat so Rosie could have a clearer view and interchanging shiny hues of purple jumped out at her.

Sunglasses might help, she thought. "Wow, that is so bright!" she said. Jimmy nodded enthusiastically. London had the best fashion, he told her, and the best clubs. London had Carnaby Street and the West End. It was the only place in the world to be. It *was* the world. And he knew she'd like it too, being a person of polish. It was full of people their age. It was alive, man. Not like here. Here was full of square rules and he couldn't wait to go.

Rosie liked him. He was adventurous. He wanted fun.

And he was generous, insisting on buying her another hot chocolate and cream slice, though his remark about lousy pocket money made her think he hadn't much to spend.

"Don't you wish things were more exciting here, Rosie?"

"Mmm."

"It'd be nice to break a few rules, wouldn't it? Boarding school is a real pain in the neck. We should hatch a plan."

Instantly a fully hatched plan leapt into her head, born of the stories she had read of long-ago boarding schools. "We could have a midnight feast in St Catherine's," she said. "Our dorm is at the top of the school. We might get away with it. You could bring David and Brian and a few more from Ivor's . . ." Even as she spoke, Rosie suspected it was the maddest idea she'd ever had.

When Jimmy seized on it she was certain.

"Genius!" he said. "Pure genius. We can get a turntable, play singles. Manfred Mann, The Rolling Stones. Jive, Twist, Rock 'n' roll. Man, we can party! Genius!"

Rosie's second thoughts were more sensible than her first. It didn't take much imagination to picture Mother Misericordia's reaction to a midnight feast, never mind a party with music and boys. Mother Misericordia would especially never recover from the presence of boys, and neither would the girls if they were caught. Still . . . there were too many rules in St Catherine's. It would be interesting to break a few of them . . .

"I don't suppose you can play the guitar?" she joked, then noting his brightening eyes, added hastily, "No. Guitars are out, Jimmy. Too loud. We'd be expelled."

They fixed on Thursday night, and worked out the details. The boys from Ivor's would get to Catherine's at a quarter to twelve on the dot. The nuns were sure to be fast asleep.

There was a lane at the back, Jimmy said, which led into the nuns' garden and the kitchens. He knew that because Father Alphonsus, his headmaster, once got him to deliver some vestments to the nuns for mending and he'd been told to use the back entrance. "He said if I went to the front door I'd only be distracted by girls. Father Alphonsus doesn't encourage girls." He grinned. "Father Alphonsus will never know how useful he's been. You can let us in the back door."

"*If* the others go for it," Rosie said. "After all, it's not my school."

"Let's find them and see."

At first the sheer nerve of the plan silenced the others. Rosie didn't try to persuade them. If they were caught she would have the least to pay. No matter what punishment Mother Misericordia devised, it wouldn't affect her after Saturday. For the others the risk was greater.

Jimmy's enthusiasm made up for her silence. "Imagine," he said, "we'll be breaking some really big rules. And we can get away with it because they're never going to think for one moment we'd do anything like this!"

Silence, then Jimmy plugged some more. "I mean, what is it anyway? It's just an ordinary, normal party and because of all their stupid, petty rules they have us thinking it's something huge. Come on, let's do it."

"We might get away with it," Katie said. "We're miles

away from the nuns' rooms and we're at the top of the school. If we're quiet . . ."

"But is Thursday the best night?" Jennie said. "We've got silent retreat all day."

Katie joined her hands and looked holy. "No one is going to think we'd have a party after a day of prayer and silence."

"It'll have to be a pyjama party," Jennie said. "We don't want to be caught dressed up in the middle of the night if there's an emergency."

They nodded.

"See," Jimmy said. "We're all sensible and we're organising a sensible party."

The boys were very keen. All the priests in Ivor's would be fast asleep an hour before they set out. Ivor's was easy to break out of. The seniors did it all the time when they wanted to have a smoke or hop down to the shops or whatever else they got up to. None of the seniors though had made the kind of history they were about to make on Thursday.

They were of one mind. The party was on.

"Fab!" Jimmy beamed at Rosie. "Really polished, man."

Rosie had put in motion one of the greatest escapades in the annals of either school.

Chapter 13

At five o'clock the three girls were the last out of the gallery. Stacia was stamping the ground, freezing and impatient, but there was nothing she could do. She wasn't keen for Mother Misericordia to discover she'd been thrown out. Her best plan, she decided bitterly, was to be as nice as possible to 2A on the way back and hope no one would say anything.

But she was raging with the three who had kept her waiting the longest. And who was Jennie O'Neill to think she could compete against her in the National Art Competition? She was full of herself, egged on by Katie McAllister and that new girl.

She really couldn't stand that new girl. Rosie McGrath showed no respect, acting as though Stacia didn't exist. She was a smart alec and not a bit shy for someone who'd been in the school only a day. Now she was thick as thieves with the other two. How did that happen? Stacia could never make friends that fast. In fact . . .

Anyhow, the girl was a pain. Mother Misericordia often

spoke of lessons in humility and how good they were for the soul. A lesson in humility was what Rosie McGrath needed. For her own good of course. In fact they all three needed to be taught some proper respect for their betters.

Sunday evening passed in a deadening routine of Study, followed by a flickering TV programme that Rosie couldn't bear to watch, a mug of cocoa with bread and jam in the refectory, and last and most tiring, the rosary in the chapel.

Mother Misericordia listened to the responses and sighed. It was obvious her students' minds were not on their prayers. Some of them were mumbling along with her, instead of answering. Others hadn't a clue which decade they were on or which Sorrowful Mystery, or even whether they should be saying the Hail Mary or the Our Father. They were hopeless. She could wake them up of course with a few choice punishments, but that would hardly make them any more devout.

Times were changing, she thought. Look at that young girl from St Aquinas, almost snoring in response. Where was the reverence and piety of the old days? She couldn't muster her usual vigorous indignation. Jennie O'Neill's sketches today had made her think for some reason about the years to come when grace and godliness might not disappear but would take on a different shape. How would she cope with such change?

The nun sighed again and took comfort in the richness of the stained-glass windows and the glow of the lamplight. "Amen," she intoned, but had to say it again before some realised the rosary was over and they could stop their inane and inaudible rumblings.

"Two announcements," Mother Misericordia was crisp. "As you know, the retreat is on Thursday. Any questions you may have for Father Hubert should be placed in this beforehand." She tapped a large square wooden box on a stand. "Secondly, the successful Child of Mary candidates will be announced on Thursday and will be invested at evening-chapel. Now to bed, please. Lights off in half an hour."

"What's a Child of Mary?" Rosie asked as they trooped upstairs.

Jennie took a deep breath and rattled Mother Misericordia's definition off by heart: "*A Child of Mary promises devotion to Our Lady; to be honest, pure of heart, obedient and hardworking; to pray for the missions and for the conversion of Russia; to resist impure thoughts; to grapple with danger and temptation and endure all suffering and affliction.*"

"Right . . ." Rosie said faintly, adding, once she'd recovered, "So obviously no one in her right mind would want to be a Child of Mary?"

"Everyone wants it," Katie told her. "Because you don't actually have to do anything, just promise."

"So, what's the point?"

"A Child of Mary stays up later on Fridays, till ten o'clock actually, gets a fry for Saturday breakfast and a pass to go into town once a week on her own, and wears a blue ribbon with a big silver medal."

"Wow!" Rosie said. "All that just for converting Russia and grappling with danger."

The others nodded solemnly.

In the dormitory Jennie and Katie, not yet pure of heart or obedient, told their classmates about the party. Some of them went into overdrive with excitement. The idea of music and boys and breaking rules was thrilling. Only one girl wasn't sure. The idea of being caught gripped her. If Old Misery found out . . . if her parents found out . . . they'd kill her. They'd think she disgraced them.

"It's only a party," Rosie said. "It won't be wild. It's not as if we've got alcohol or drugs. There's not going to be a big crowd either, and only a few boys. We won't even have great music."

"But . . . *boys*," said the girl. She might as well have said "*aliens*".

Then Jennie said the whole dorm had to agree because if they were caught they'd all be blamed.

They held their breath. The girl looked at their expectant faces and couldn't bear to be a spoilsport. She changed her mind but still looked worried until Jennie promised that if they were caught they'd tell Mother Misericordia she had been against it from the start. That might save her.

Within half an hour Stacia Bolger arrived to check they were all in bed. The prefect put the lights out and closed the door, lingering to make sure there was no talking. Once her footsteps creaked away they chatted for a while longer, deciding what records they'd play, what party food they could muster, how they could rearrange the room for dancing.

At last the talk petered out and one by one they dropped off to sleep.

Later, sometime in the middle of the night, a cold draught swept through the room and the curtains rustled as the door groaned on its hinges. A white figure hovered for a moment then moved across the dormitory towards the alcove.

Rosie dreamed.

A white bare branch rapped on the open window, reached through the curtains into the room and tapped across the floorboards like a blind man's cane. In her dream the branch touched her shoulder and curled around her neck, cold as death. Her breath caught at the icy sensation. She choked, gasped and woke. Above her a white figure loomed and Rosie screamed. The shape retreated silently and disappeared.

"Who screamed? What's happening?"

"What's going on?"

"It's freezing in here. Who opened the door?"

Katie got up and put on the light. Girls rubbed their eyes, cross and scared as they tried to figure out what happened. A gale swept from the open window across the room and out through the open door. The sash knocked insistently against the frame and the curtains billowed out. Katie closed the door and someone else pulled down the window.

"Sorry I screamed," Rosie said. "Someone was standing by my bed and there was a tapping noise. I thought I was freezing to death."

Some of the girls looked at each other and one asked, "What was the figure like? Was it a ghost?"

"Of course it wasn't a ghost," Jennie said briskly. "It was a bad dream. The window was rattling and the room was freezing. No wonder Rosie had a nightmare."

"But how did the door open?"

"Don't be such a ninny!" Jennie said. "It blew open because no one closed the window. Ghosts don't need to open doors. They can glide through them." Then she made a sudden wavering noise, "*Whooooooo!*"

Katy threw a pillow at her. She threw it back and soon others joined in and normality was restored.

Rosie drew the bedclothes around her. A nightmare was the only explanation, she thought. She didn't believe in ghosts, and a figure didn't appear and disappear unless it was part of a dream.

Still, when the lights went out she kept her eyes shut-tight for fear of what she might see and it was a long time before the white shape faded from her mind and sleep came again.

Chapter 14

"I want to talk to you." Stacia Bolger planted herself in front of Jennie. It was after breakfast and the girls were making their way to class.

"You two," she waved at Rosie and Katie, "go away!"

Jennie gripped her friends' elbows. "They're not going anywhere and you can't speak to people like that."

Stacia forced herself to smile and be polite. "I'm sorry," she said. "I didn't mean to be rude."

What game was this? Astounded, they waited.

"I want to talk about the Art competition." Stacia looked around. They were the only group now on the corridor. "You know my father, John Bolger, is an artist? *The* John Bolger, actually."

Their faces told her they'd never heard of him and Stacia swallowed her annoyance. "It doesn't matter," she said. "It's just that Art is very important to him. Last year in the competition I got a distinction and Miss Madden says I've improved immensely since then and have a great chance this year – Miss Madden is the Art teacher," she added for Rosie's benefit.

Jennie nodded, wondering where this was leading and the older girl saw she would have to spell it out.

"Last year's winner was older than me and so was everyone else who got a distinction. They've all left school, so they can't enter this year. With them out of the way, I'm the best."

Suddenly Rosie understood. "You want Jennie not to enter," she said.

The girl ignored her, focussing on Jennie. "You don't have to send in a picture this year. You've got plenty of time, four more chances before you leave. I've seen your work." She stopped, waiting, but the others said nothing, shocked at Stacia's brass neck.

"'A good draughtswoman,' Miss Madden calls me," the prefect continued. "She'd no idea you were entering the competition when she said this was my chance. I'd like to be an artist like my father."

What Stacia didn't say was that she needed to prove herself. Her father wanted her to be the best and had no time for the second-rate. Distinctions weren't good enough. First prize was all that mattered.

Jennie knew now what the senior wanted her to do. For once she felt sorry for the other girl, but her thoughts were clear. "You could win, Stacia, no matter who enters. But you can't be the best just by getting rid of anyone else who might have a chance."

"You've a nerve to ask," Katie said.

"Too right," Rosie added her support.

Stacia's face flooded with colour at their scorn. Flattery and niceness had got her nowhere and she would not use them again. Without another word she turned and left them.

They got into class some minutes after first bell but seconds ahead of the teacher. Rosie expected to be completely bewildered by Maths, especially if the questions involved pounds, shillings and pence, but the topic was Algebra, which was as old as the hills, and she managed the problems quite well.

The morning passed without difficulty. The only subject Rosie had never done before was Nature Study. She thought it quaint, to do with pressed flowers and leaves and drawing robins and squirrels and learning about their habits. Rosie's robin was very lopsided, as if it had keeled over from drink. It was also much too large. She went into a pleasant trance colouring it and the end product was overall bright scarlet. She tried to add some greys and brown but the result was sad. Miss Enfield, a gentle, elderly lady, looked amused and said it was like a moulting parrot.

In Religion they paid little attention as the amiable and restful Mother Clementine read the parables. Instead they silently passed notes around, planning the party in minute detail.

Rosie learned quickly that teachers in St Catherine's were used to obedience and respect. Even the most tedious lesson hardly provoked a murmur of restlessness. In her own school a boring class could produce at best a coma and at worst pandemonium. Now she got used to standing up every time a teacher came into the room, to the prayer before class, to standing up again when class was over to join in the chorus of "Thank you, Miss". What she couldn't get used to was the fact that someone always volunteered to carry the teacher's books from one class to the next. It was a bit like having a personal slave, but since no one else seemed to notice the terrible imposition, she kept her thoughts to herself.

Rosie didn't get into trouble once, which would've been a miracle in her own school, never mind this one. But then, she'd never been on her best behaviour in CCS. Being perfect was a terrible strain and she was glad when the morning was over.

In the refectory Rosie saw that Stacia seemed to have a new friend. They huddled together at the sixth-year table, keen to keep their conversation private. Every so often they raised their heads and looked towards 2A. Catching Rosie's eye, the girl looked hostile. It was clear Stacia had an ally.

That afternoon at Art, Miss Madden complimented Jennie on her sketches. "They're very promising and your idea is so interesting. I presume you'll use watercolours."

"I'd like to use oils, Miss. They're richer and they'll give me the right atmosphere."

"But you've only got this week left, Jennie. You could ruin your painting if you don't allow each layer to dry out before applying the next one and oils take a lot longer."

Jennie thought. "It can be done in three layers, Miss. Maybe I will ruin the painting, but I'd like to try oils."

"Well then, I've got the canvas for you. It's already stretched and tacked and a good size. I was going to use it for my own work, but this is more important. Have a look."

Miss Madden and Jennie went off into a small storage room. The rest of the class continued with their still-life drawings. Their desks surrounded a central table on which was placed a patterned dish full of fruit. Soon Jennie was busy setting up, and the teacher was busy helping her. Miss Madden had no time to give to the new girl and Rosie was grateful. Art certainly wasn't her strong subject. She thought of Dad and how he joked about her progress.

She felt a surge of homesickness. Mum and Dad were going about their lives thinking their only daughter was in Cork. Helena would have texted them, of that she was sure. Helena was a good friend. She'd like Jennie, as a girl that is. It would be different meeting her only as a middle-aged woman.

After Rosie had met Gran as a girl in 1920, she no longer thought of her just as an old lady. Ever since then she could see the person Gran had been when she was young and now and then when Gran said, "Sometimes, inside, I'm still twelve years old," Rosie understood exactly.

At Study that evening Rosie did her best with the homework, even copying out her letter to Patrick to use as her English essay. With time over she looked at Gray's 'Elegy'.

An hour or so later the shadows on the dim corridors and stairs made her think of graveyards and ghosts. She was the first into the dormitory and as she groped for the light switch she could see the outline of every bed except her own. The alcove where she slept was black as the grave. Hurriedly she pressed the switch and was relieved to see the darkness disappear.

Chapter 15

For a while after lights-out that night little disturbed the silence in the dormitory. The odd snuffle and snore and the creak of old floorboards faded into the darkness. There was no wind. Moonlight filtered through a gap in the heavy curtains, running in a silver line along the floor. All across the sky millions of stars lit the frozen night like faraway, tiny icicles.

The figure made no noise. No breathing whitened the crisp air and even the floorboards were still. The pale form drew close to the alcove and leaning over the sleeping girl, seemed to smooth the heavy quilt near her face, then straightened up and moved away, turning back once when Rosie groaned in her sleep. But the girl didn't wake and in another second the figure was gone.

Next morning Rosie woke to the clanging bell. Stacia was swinging it with all her strength. None of their protests had any effect. For five minutes she clanged, though they were out of bed in a jiffy, hands over their ears and groaning in misery. Even after she left, their jarred nerves went on clanging until the air finally stopped reverberating.

"She'd wake the dead, that one," Katie said, still clutching her head.

Rosie caught her breath at a faint memory. She recalled half waking with the cold and saw again a form drifting away towards the door. Then she had drifted off into slumber. I'd hardly have slept again if I'd just seen a ghost, she thought. I must have been dreaming.

Unbidden came the memory of someone leaning right over her. She turned towards her bed looking for a trace. On the other side of the pillow was a magazine, its pages curling with age. After a moment she reached over, then hesitated, unable to explain her reluctance. If someone in the dormitory wanted to give her a magazine, they'd have handed it to her, not mysteriously left it on her bed in the middle of the night.

Convincing herself there was nothing to fear from an old magazine, Rosie picked it up:

The Lanthorn, January 1954
St Catherine's School Journal

It opened at page 58 and she saw a black and white photograph of a schoolgirl about her own age. She was dark-haired, her face delicate and pensive, mouth upturned, not quite smiling. Serious, but not unhappy, Rosie thought, certain even before she saw the name that this was Caroline Browne. Underneath she read:

The Sad Loss of Caroline Browne

Just a few weeks ago, in December, St Catherine's lost one of its most engaging students. Caroline Browne's untimely death at the age of thirteen came as an appalling shock to her family and to all in the school. Caroline's health was never good and tragically she succumbed to pneumonia.

During her last days, she was preoccupied with the loss of a sapphire ring, a gift from her grandmother who died last July. This was an heirloom, passed down for two hundred years to the youngest female member of the family. It was something she treasured, more for its family history than its value, and she fretted greatly when the ring disappeared.

In spite of a thorough search of St Catherine's, and especially of the dormitory and the alcove where Caroline slept, the item has not yet been found but we have assured her parents that the search for this precious memento will continue.

During the one term she was with us, Caroline revealed a thoughtful character that initially hid a talent for mischief. As her classmates got to know her she emerged from her shyness and showed a great gift for mimicry. She imitated her teachers' quirks with an accuracy which even they found comic.

Caroline was much liked by staff and students and is greatly missed.

Requiescat in pacem.

Rosie sighed. Stacia Bolger must have put the magazine beside her pillow, as proof that a student had died here, in this bed, ten years ago, trying to convince her that Caroline's ghost was haunting her. Remembering the prefect's bitter expression yesterday, Rosie knew she was mean enough to act like a ghost, to appear in the middle of the night and leave a reminder of the dead girl. And she did it because Rosie had more or less called her a fool.

The prefect's plan was to frighten her and it wasn't going to work. Rosie put the magazine in her bedside locker. After breakfast she waited outside the refectory. Stacia emerged with her crony of yesterday and Rosie smiled sweetly.

"Oh, Stacia, I so want to thank you for the magazine." Stacia glared at her. "Sorry?"

"*The Lanthorn, 1954.* I read about Caroline Browne. She wasn't a bit like you said. I think you thought she was boring, but actually she was great fun, really interesting. If I had to be haunted by someone, I don't think I'd mind a ghost like her." Rosie smiled again and sauntered off.

"What's she talking about?" Stacia's companion said. "She sounds unhinged." She glanced at Stacia, "Unless you've been up to something? Have you?"

"She'll be unhinged by the time I've finished with her," Stacia fumed. "I promise you that, Delia. Her and Jennie O'Neill."

Delia smiled slyly. "What a pity Jennie is a better artist than you. Otherwise there'd be no contest. You'd easily win."

"It's not that she's better." Stacia's face tightened at the notion. "She's original all right, and some of the judges love that. If they see paint thrown at the canvas, they think it's original." She noticed Delia's amused grin and her eyes narrowed. "My work is far superior, but then you don't know much about painting, do you? You don't know much about anything."

Her companion's smile vanished. "I know you need my help. I know that much."

At once Stacia became friendly again, "And next week you can cog off me at the Christmas exams – that's the bargain. I'll make sure you pass everything."

"You'd better." The other girl was still sullen.

"Of course I will," Stacia said. "After all, I don't want you snitching on me to Mother Misericordia."

The other girl's face brightened immediately as she saw the hold she would have over the prefect.

Stacia was satisfied. Really, Delia was incredibly stupid not to realise if she said anything to Old Misery she'd be landing herself in trouble.

There was no way Stacia was going to let her cog even one test. They were bound to be caught, not least because Delia would make a hames of it. Then they'd be disgraced and it didn't take much imagination to guess how her father would react. No. Cogging was out of the question, not that she'd let Delia know till between them they'd destroyed her rival's chances.

She smiled as warmly as she knew how at Delia. "We have to make sure Jennie O'Neill gets into so much trouble she's not allowed to represent the school in the art competition. Now here's the plan . . ."

Chapter 16

Every Tuesday morning 2A did gym for an hour. However, this Tuesday the gym teacher told Jennie she was excused. "Miss Madden wants you in the Art room. She says you need the time to get your painting finished. So off with you now. Leave your bag where it is and one of your friends will take it to class."

Delighted with the extra time, Jennie flew.

Some time later, while 2A was playing indoor basketball, Delia Waters sneaked into the cloakroom next to the gym and, after some checking, found Jennie's bag and picked out her English copy. Carefully she took off the brown-paper cover, put it on the copy she had brought and dropped this in the satchel. Making sure nothing looked disturbed, she left.

Ellen the maid, dusting the statue of St Dominic in his alcove was surprised to see Delia Waters sneaking down the basement stairs, past the kitchen and towards the back door, something rolled up in her hand. None of the students ever came this way unless they were on an errand.

It was clear Delia wasn't on an errand. From the look of her she didn't want to be seen.

Ellen's curiosity got the better of her and she went to the top of the stairs.

The senior darted out the door and back in. Taken by surprise at her speed, Ellen barely had time to turn back around the corner and into the alcove. Delia's hands were empty and the maid was curious.

A few minutes later, Ellen was looking around the winter garden, at the bare trees, the frosted paths, the glinting clay of the flower-beds. Even the grass was stiff with cold and she could imagine it crunching underfoot, but the only footprints led to a huge bin which was full of kitchen waste and due for collection at eleven o'clock.

Lifting the lid, the maid immediately saw the copy. There was no name on it and she couldn't figure out why Delia Waters would go to such trouble when she could have thrown it into any old wastepaper basket. Earlier that morning she'd seen Delia and Stacia whispering. There was something funny going on and, if the sixth-year prefect was involved, it was bound to be sneaky. Ellen took the copy.

Jennie was pleased with her picture. She was working fast and already the background was almost finished – the sky, the street, some of the buildings. "You've brought me luck," she said, taking her satchel from Rosie just before English. "This is the first time I've been able to see an entire painting in my head before I started. Usually I can't make up my mind what I want to do and the picture keeps changing as I paint. Sometimes it's a mess, but not this one."

Locky collected their essays and set them the task of reading Stave One in *A Christmas Carol*. "You'll have some questions for homework, so pay close attention to the text. Not a whisper do I want to hear. I'm going to correct your work, so absolute silence, please. Rosie, take my copy of the novel."

Rosie loved reading and the first sentence drew her in: "*Marley was dead, to begin with.*" In no time she was hooked. So were they all. No one made a sound, absorbed by the icy nature of Marley's living partner, Scrooge: "*Hard and sharp as flint . . . The cold within him froze his old features, nipped his pointed nose, shrivelled his cheek . . .*" Scrooge was a man who edged his way "*along the crowded paths of life, warning all human sympathy to keep its distance*".

Every so often Miss Lockhart looked up from her work and surveyed them. They were engrossed and no one caught her eye. Outside the sky was again heavy with snow and quietly the teacher crossed the room to switch on the light. Not a head turned.

The ceiling lamp barely lifted the gloom. The dim light was more ghostly than darkness. In such an atmosphere Rosie's nerves were taut as she read of the fog that thickened the London air outside Marley's office and "the piercing, searching, biting cold" that entered his bones, chilled her too.

Arriving home, Scrooge saw Marley's ghostly face on his front door and was for a moment terrified. So was Rosie, as Marley's hair stirred and his wide-open eyes remained motionless. She swallowed hard when Scrooge entered his house and saw a hearse before him in the gloom.

And at the point where heavy chains clanked across the cellar and Scrooge remembered hearing that ghosts in haunted houses were described as dragging chains – just at that point – Miss Lockhart rapped the table with her pen and Rosie shrieked with fright. She wasn't the only one and the teacher found herself looking at faces that were almost as livid as the dead Marley's.

Miss Lockhart's face, on the other hand, was blazing. "Jennie O'Neill," she said, her voice shaking with the effort to control her anger, "Jennie O'Neill, after class you will explain precisely why you wrote this offensive essay." Her voice rose, "Never in my whole teaching life has any girl been so insulting!"

Jennie's mouth dropped open and the teacher waved a hand, "This is not for discussion now. I'm not about to parade this outrage in public. After class, please."

Looking at the girl's shocked face, Rosie could see she had no notion what had so offended the teacher. Now the silence that descended had nothing to do with Dickens's story. Every girl knew Jennie was in serious trouble and, although they bowed their heads again, none of them read a word, waiting for the bell to break some of the suspense, for then at least, even if they didn't know what was going on, they could talk about it. They were dying to talk about it. No one in her right mind would cross Locky and they shivered for Jennie.

When class was over the teacher strode from the class,

indicating with an imperious nod that Jennie was to follow.

"I'll go with you," Rosie said.

"Thanks, but that's not a good idea. She'd eat you."

Others in the class murmured their sympathy. Outside Jennie heard the buzz of conversation that broke behind her. Ahead she saw Miss Lockhart making for the principal's office and, heart sinking, she followed.

"Are you all right, Jennie?"

Ellen was on her way to the nuns' staffroom with a tray for Mother Clementine, who liked to mark her breaks with pots of tea and biscuits. "Afraid not," Jennie groaned. "I'm in trouble with Miss Lockhart over my essay, but I don't know why she's so raging. She says she never read anything so insulting! I don't understand. It's only a stupid story about the future and she doesn't even come into it."

Miss Lockhart was waiting impatiently at the office and Jennie speeded up, not wanting to give more offence.

"Mother Misericordia is on her way," the teacher sniffed, ushering them both into the office. "While we're waiting, please explain yourself." As if it were a piece of dirt, she dropped the copy on the principal's table and Jennie picked it up.

She couldn't understand it. Her name was on the cover. It looked like her English copy, but what was written inside was beyond her understanding. Line after line on page after page described the English teacher as the meanest, most malicious person ever known. She was a tyrant who loved punishing people. She got girls to learn millions of verses of stupid poems and gave them detention for missing a line. She was horrible and everyone was afraid of her and she was a terrible teacher. Not only that, she was ugly and badly dressed and hated by all her classes. And so on and on . . .

"I can't believe this," the teacher fumed.

"Neither can I," Jennie whispered.

Ellen the maid, meanwhile, had also speeded up. She practically ran all the way to the nun's staffroom and when Mother Clementine opened the door to her insistent knocking, she pushed the tray at her and said, "Sorry, Mother. I'm in a terrible rush. Will you pour the tea for yourself today?"

Then she was gone, racing to the cleaners' storeroom where she'd left the copy she'd found in the dustbin. Quickly she turned the pages and when she came to a story called, 'The Future' she zoomed off at once.

Two minutes later she knocked on the principal's office and barged into the middle of an argument.

"Of course you did it. It's your copy," Miss Lockhart was saying.

"But it's not my writing!" By now Jennie sounded just as definite as the teacher. "And I'd never write anything like that."

"I am no expert on calligraphy," said Miss Lockhart, "but as far as I can see it resembles your writing. In any case, you're not denying it's your copy? Your name is on the cover."

"I only know I didn't write all that rubbish, Miss – and that's a new copy. My copy isn't new. There's loads of other work in it."

Neither noticed the maid standing there. Ellen waved

the copy and coughed loudly but she remained invisible until she shouted, "Miss Lockhart, Miss Lockhart! She's right. It's not her copy. This is hers."

Locky glared at the interference and swiped the copy from her. Quickly she went through it while Jennie stared, bewildered. Unmistakably, this was Jennie's work. The teacher recognised the exercises she'd set. The answers and the marks given were all Jennie's. She compared the writing in both copies and saw that, though similar, the offending pages were in someone else's hand.

Taking a deep breath Miss Lockhart turned to Jennie. "I'm sorry. I'm not good on handwriting and I've made a terrible mistake."

Jennie gulped, "It's not your fault, Miss. It's my cover but I've no idea why it's on that copy. You made a genuine mistake, Miss."

"That's very good of you," Miss Lockhart said, "very decent." Especially, she thought, as she'd wanted to strangle the girl a moment ago. She turned to the maid, "Where did you find Jennie's copy?"

"In the bin outside the kitchen, Miss."

Jennie frowned. "How on earth did it get there? I didn't throw it out."

Ellen said nothing. Afterwards she would tell the second-year what had happened, but not now, not in front of Miss Lockhart. Stacia would kill her if she snitched to a teacher.

Locky broke the silence. "Someone has been playing a nasty trick on us both, Jennie, and now that I've had time to think, I'm sure it's no one in 2A."

"So am I, Miss." Eagerly Jennie defended the class. "No one thinks you're that rotten, Miss . . . sorry, I don't mean that you're even a bit rotten. I mean –"

Locky smiled. "It's all right. Now you two better leave me to deal with Mother Misericordia. She'll be looking for an explanation. And, Ellen, you did a great job. Thank you."

Outside the office, Ellen told her story. Jennie could hardly believe it. Stacia Bolger must hate her to organise something so vicious. "If it wasn't for you, I'd be in such trouble, maybe even expelled. Then I'd never get to enter the competition . . . Thanks, Ellen, you got me out of an awful mess."

"You watch out for her, Miss. She's nasty. Oh my God, you didn't see me! I'm out of here!" She disappeared up the stairs.

Down the corridor towards them came Mother Clementine. Gone was her usual gentle expression. Instead she had a face like thunder. "Ellen! Come back at once, Ellen! You threw that pot of tea right over me."

Jennie too decided it was time to disappear and Mother Clementine found she was shouting into an empty corridor.

Chapter 17

The moment Stacia saw Jennie in the refectory at lunchtime she knew her plan had failed. The second-year should have been in disgrace, possibly in solitary confinement for hours, with time to contemplate her misdeeds before being suspended or even expelled and considered unfit to represent the school.

Mother Misericordia was fond of solitary confinement for big crimes and there was no doubt in Stacia's mind that insulting one of the most respected teachers in the school with such vitriol would be high on the principal's list of criminal activities.

So what was Jennie O'Neill doing, happily eating her dinner and smiling away? Stacia couldn't help staring across as she tried to work out what had gone wrong. Jennie and her friends stared back and smiled triumphantly. The new girl from Quinos waved and said something to the others that made them laugh. The senior flushed and turned away. "You're useless, Delia Waters, absolutely useless!" she snarled at her companion.

"It's not my fault she's still here. I did exactly what you said so don't blame me."

"I do blame you and you won't be getting any help from me in your exams. The deal's off."

Resentfully, both retreated into silence, brooding on failure.

Finally Delia said bitterly, "I switched copies and put hers in the bin, exactly like you said. It's not my fault."

"Maybe not," Stacia agreed, busy plotting again. "Did anyone see you?"

"Don't think so. I saw someone though. That little maid. She's harmless and never noticed me."

"I bet she did. Anyway, never mind. I have another plan. We need your brother, though. You'll have to call him."

Delia didn't like the sound of this. It was one thing for her to help Stacia, quite another to involve her brother. And as the prefect revealed the plot her misgivings grew. "He'll never do that." She was aghast.

"He will if you want to get through your exams."

Delia lapsed into sullen silence. Perhaps exams weren't so important.

"Just imagine your report," Stacia said. "Imagine getting a good mark in every subject. Imagine your parents, how they'll feel."

Usually Delia's parents were reluctant to open her reports. When they did, Delia couldn't bear their disappointment. Once she overheard her mother wonder why they were spending so much money on her education. Delia sighed. It would be nice if for once she didn't have to go through the same old rigmarole and feel stupid and ashamed as they read her results. When it came to exams, everything she ever knew in every subject vanished in a kind of panic. Just once it would be great to get an excellent report.

"Okay, okay. I'll make him do it," Delia said. "He's going out with a girl my parents don't like. He'd hate them to know . . ." She got on well with her older brother but quickly put aside the thought that he might not be so fond of her after this.

Later Stacia saw Ellen carrying a pile of sheets upstairs. She caught up with her on the second landing. "I want a word with you," she said and before the maid knew what was happening the prefect had upended the sheets onto the floor and pushed her against the wall, bruising her hip. "Don't you interfere in my business again," she told her. "Do you hear me? Do you?"

"Yes." The maid cowered, wishing she were bigger and stronger and braver and could stand up to bullies instead of immediately collapsing.

Stacia smacked her face, catching the corner of her eye with her thumbnail. The maid's whimpering cry gave her great satisfaction as she strode away.

Painfully Ellen gathered the linen, limped up to 2A's dormitory and began the task of changing the sheets. She was slower than usual and when Rosie came in an hour later to deposit some books, Ellen was still there, making the beds.

"You were brilliant today," Rosie told her. "Jennie told me what you did." Then she saw the girl's face, "What happened your eye? God, it looks sore!"

Saying what happened would cause more trouble, Ellen reckoned. "I slipped on the stairs," she said and some hesitation in the answer told the other girl this wasn't true.

"No, you didn't. Look at you. Your face is swollen. You didn't just slip on the stairs. What happened?"

The combination of violent shock and Rosie's sympathy weakened the maid's defences. Suddenly she was weeping and telling everything.

Rosie was outraged. "We can't let her get away with it!"

Overcome by the notion that she wasn't on her own, hearing that word "we", Ellen sobbed her heart out. Eventually the sobs became snuffles, then hiccups. When she was cried-out, she said, "I don't see what we can do. I'm not going to tell Mother Misericordia. That'd be snitching. Telling you is different."

Rosie considered. Everyone liked and trusted the young maid, everyone except Stacia Bolger. But that would change if Ellen ratted, even on someone as horrible as the sixth-year. Nobody would talk to her which would make working in St Catherine's impossible.

"I'll think of something," she said, not at all sure that she would.

At tea she told Jennie and Katie what had happened.

"That girl has to be stopped," Katie said, her angry voice carrying. "Look what she did this morning, and now this. She doesn't care about anyone."

All talk at the table died down. It was obvious from her red face that Katie was furious and 2A wanted to know why. Katie started to tell them, her indignation loud.

"Keep your voice down," Jennie urged. "We've no proof and Stacia knows that. She'll kick up no end if she hears you."

Katie lowered her voice and continued. The class had been trying to find out all day what had lit Locky's fuse and now they heard. But Stacia's treatment of the young maid shocked them more. Although there was no proof, except Ellen's word, they had no doubts. No one liked Stacia and no one tried to defend her.

At the end of Katie's tale not a word was said.

Glancing across, the prefect shifted uneasily as all of 2A silently stared at her.

Chapter 18

That night Rosie couldn't sleep. Her mind ranged over all that was happening.

The one big drawback to school, she'd always thought, was attending class. Homework too, but that was easier to avoid than class, where you had to put up with subjects you didn't like and teachers who expected you to work. School would be wonderful without teachers. She'd said as much once in CCS to Ms Henry, when the Art teacher wanted more of an effort. The words had slipped out in irritation because Ms Henry was picking on her. She'd expected a right telling-off, but the teacher had sighed and her face had looked dreamy and she'd said, "Or even better, Rosie – what about school without students? Imagine the peace and calm. I could get on with my own work and drop into the staffroom now and again for a chat and a coffee. Bliss." Then she'd given herself a shake and added, "Yes, well, there's no perfection in this life – and especially not in your dismal efforts. So more application, please."

But in St Catherine's, strangely, Rosie was having no

problems with class, even today in Latin. Maybe it was because she'd said nothing, paid close attention in case she got caught out and avoided Minnie's eye so she wouldn't be asked any questions. In Rosie's experience, looking directly at teachers only drew their attention. So, except for the terrible strain of keeping quiet, class was no problem. Neither was homework because Jennie gave her all the help she needed.

But one colossal problem was Stacia Bolger – a dangerous person when she didn't get her own way, even to someone caught in the middle, like Ellen.

But at least 2A had shown exactly what they thought of her. When Stacia had turned up at the dormitory for 'Lights Out', everyone had gone silent. As usual she'd harangued them, telling them to get a move on and hurry up into bed. She gave out about clothes being left on the floor and she switched the light on and off a number of times.

But, unusually, no one protested. Silently the clothes were tidied away. Silently they got into bed. Silently they put up with the on-and-off light. Stacia was bemused. She flicked the switch for the last time, "Good night then," she said. Nothing. She repeated, "I said goodnight. Are you all deaf?" No one answered. Having waited a moment, she muttered, "Have it your own way," and was gone.

After today it was obvious Stacia thought the best way to keep Jennie out of the Art competition was to get her suspended or expelled. The silent treatment from 2A wouldn't stop her. She was bound to have another plan and they would have to watch out.

Rosie knew she was included in Stacia's dislike. That was why the prefect had tried to frighten her and why she'd left the magazine on her bed. Poor Caroline Browne, Rosie thought. Imagine fretting about an old ring when she was so ill. Had it ever been found? It must have been very precious. Such a sad story.

Sad . . . so sad . . . sad . . . Rosie was almost asleep when suddenly Stacia's words came to mind: *The searcher looked up and saw a deathly figure at a high window in the storeroom in the corridor outside this dormitory . . .*

Why had Caroline been in that room? Was it where she'd lost the ring? Why else would she have gone there?

Wide awake now, Rosie pondered the possibility until it became a certainty. She would have to look and the best time was now, with everyone asleep and no one likely to ask where she was or what she was doing.

Swiftly, so that she wouldn't think about it too much, Rosie got out of bed. The door creaked as she opened and closed it, but no one woke.

The storeroom was pitch-black until she switched on the light. The dim glow made the darkness patchy and created huge shadows. It was a horrible room. The window at the far end made it more ghostly, gleaming dully without casting any light. Rosie was tempted to turn back. Maybe the ring had been found in the ten years since Caroline's death and this search was a waste of time. But what if it hadn't been found?

She made up her mind. She would start by the window and work back. Making her way past the old chairs and desks, past shelves and cupboards, Rosie clambered over an old sofa and was almost there when she tripped and gripped one of the curtains. The ancient fabric came away from the rail and enveloped her. Shrouded in dust and cloth, Rosie was terrified, unable to breathe. The more she struggled the more caught up she became. She tried to cry out but the sound emerged as a strangled cough.

"Sssss . . ." she heard, "sssss . . ."

More frantic than ever she grappled with the cloth and at last and with a great deal of luck she was free.

"Sssss . . ." she heard the hissing again, "sssss . . ." But she could see no one. It would be easy for someone to hide in the gloom, to crouch down behind the furniture and pounce as she was leaving.

The sound came again and this time a slight breeze touched her face.

It's just the air from the window, she thought with relief and to prove it she held a hand over the sash and a breath sighed through the gap.

Her courage revived enough to search under furniture and behind the cushions on the sofa. Then she looked up and saw shadows all the length of the room, moving as if in wait and her heart jolted in fright. She couldn't stay one more second.

Rosie clambered back to the door and was up the corridor and into the dorm in record time.

Tomorrow, she decided, pulling the blankets around her, I'll find out if that ring was found. If it wasn't I'll get Jennie and Katie to help me look. And I'll use a torch. One thing for sure, I'm never going back there on my own!

Chapter 19

At breakfast on Wednesday Stacia Bolger tested her suspicion that no one in 2A was talking to her by saying a loud "Good morning!" at their table. There was no response. Fine, she thought, at least there'll be no stupid complaints.

"You, Jennie O'Neill," she said, "I'm on library duty first lesson so before class I want you to collect 2A's library books and bring them to me, with a list of borrowers, and the date each book is due back. Understand?"

Jennie was silent. The rest of the class glared at Stacia but said nothing. The prefect sauntered off, smiling, knowing well the second-year would now be dead late for class and in trouble.

"That girl has a big problem," Rosie said.

"No, I have a big problem," Jennie told her. "By the time everyone finds their books and I fill in a list, I'm going to be really late for English. I don't want any more trouble with Locky after yesterday, but neither do I want Stacia to report me."

"That prefect hates you," one of the girls said. "It's not fair."

The class sank into a glum silence, meditating on the sixth-year's meanness.

Then Katie had an idea. "Rosie didn't borrow any books so she doesn't have to run around looking for them. Once we find ours, she can take down the information Stacia wants on a blank page. It will save you time, Jennie."

So, as soon as breakfast was finished, they fetched their library books while Rosie headed an A4 page:

Names	*Titles*	*Date*

List completed, there was still time before first class. She and Jennie were on their way to the library with a satchel of books when Miss Madden stopped them.

"Mother Misericordia says you may work on your painting this morning, Jennie," the Art teacher said, "You're excused class. Come along."

"I've to leave these books back to the library first, Miss."

"I'm sure Rosie can do that. There's no time to waste."

Rosie took the books. "Don't worry about anything except the painting," she said.

Jennie smiled gratefully and followed the Art teacher.

Now, where's the library? Rosie wondered. The class-bell rang out and the corridors cleared before she could ask anyone. Hesitating and pondering, she didn't notice Mother Misericordia until the nun was in front of her.

"Why are you not in class, girl?"

"I'm looking for the library, Mother."

"If I'm not mistaken, 2A's library session is on Friday afternoon, not first thing on Wednesday morning."

"But Stacia Bolger wants all the books back right now, Mother."

"Did *she* tell you that? Surely not. She knows the rules." Mother Misericordia was disbelieving. It was obvious to her that the new girl was trying to skip class.

"No, she didn't tell *me* that," Rosie wanted to be precise. "It was Jennie O'Neill she told. She said Jennie was to collect all the books with a list of names and return dates. But you said Jennie could go to Art, and she's gone off with Miss Madden so I'm taking the books instead, only I don't know where the library is and when the bell rang everyone disappeared before I –"

Mother Misericordia put up a hand, feeling tired and not wanting to listen to any more. "*I* will take the books," she said. "*You* go to class."

Happily Rosie handed over the satchel and the list. Then she thought of something. "Can I ask you a question, Mother?"

Mother Misericordia sighed. "If it's not a long question."

"I was reading about Caroline Browne, the girl who died ten years ago in our dormitory. She died in my bed actually, I think. So Stacia says. Anyway she lost a sapphire ring and I was wondering if it was ever found. Was it, Mother? That's my question."

The nun was startled into silence. Where did Rosie read about the dead girl? Why did Stacia Bolger, prefect and mentor to 2A, tell such a thing to a new girl? And how did Rosie feel about it? But Mother Misericordia was a very busy woman and the answers to these questions could well be long and complicated. I'll ask some other time, she thought.

"Well, dear," she said at last, "I wasn't here ten years ago and although I've heard of Caroline Browne I don't know anything about a ring. But you could always ask Mother Benedicta." Seeing Rosie's puzzlement she added, "You may not have met her. She's Caroline's older sister and teaches German to the senior classes. Now off to class at once, please."

Oh damn, Stacia Bolger thought when Mother Misericordia entered the library. Stacia was looking forward to Jennie O'Neill's arrival and had thought of various ways to delay the girl. She wanted to show Jennie how stupid it was to cross her, that this was only a tiny example of how she, Stacia, could make her life a misery. But she couldn't do that if the principal was hanging around.

"Good morning, Mother." Her smile was obsequious.

The head nun put the bag of books on a table. "I believe you wanted these from 2A, as well as this list." She handed the page to Stacia.

"Well, I – yes, I suppose – but I didn't mean for you . . ." She couldn't hold the nun's steadfast gaze.

Mother Misericordia knew that look. It happened only when a girl was caught out doing something she shouldn't be doing. Stacia Bolger looked guilty.

"You have responsibilities as prefect, Stacia, and you're supposed to set an example to 2A, not lead them astray by making them miss class."

The prefect nodded in perfect agreement and smiled weakly, mentally noting that Jennie O'Neill must have snitched on her. She would pay for this big time.

"I also think it's highly irresponsible," Mother Misericordia continued in glacial tones, "to tell a vulnerable newcomer that she is sleeping in a dead person's bed. This is not the behaviour expected of St Catherine's prefects."

Vulnerable? Rosie McGrath?

"No, Mother. I'm very sorry, Mother. It won't happen again." And it wouldn't. She'd make sure neither of them would ever want to snitch again.

"Your apology may well be too late," the principal sniffed. "I will have to review your position as prefect."

Stacia was truly dismayed. Being a prefect made her feel important, not just in school, but at home. When her father heard she was considered responsible enough for the honour he'd been so pleased. "Well done, Stacia! You're standing out from the crowd," he'd said. If that honour was taken from her she'd be one of the crowd again, dull and ordinary, and she dreaded to think of his disappointment.

Mother Misericordia saw the girl's distress. "You know, Stacia, one of the reasons I made you prefect was because you wanted it so much. I thought you'd do everything in your power to merit the honour. Now you have to put these mistakes behind you and prove me right."

Stacia didn't quite understand. Was she still a prefect?

"You're getting another chance," the principal confirmed. "Use it well."

"I will, Mother. Oh, I will."

And she would. Without troublemakers like Jennie

O'Neill and her two friends, she could be a great prefect. Well, a phone call should see the back of Jennie. And when the other two realised Stacia was behind her expulsion they'd be very careful not to oppose her again. She'd be a great prefect all right. Soon.

Chapter 20

At lunchtime Ellen came running into the refrectory. "Where's Jennie O'Neill. Mother Misericordia says there's a phone call for her. Where is she?"

"Still in the Art room," Rosie said.

"It's urgent," Ellen said. "She'll be ages getting to the phone from the Art room. Can you take it, Rosie? It's her cousin, Alan . . . a family matter."

Rosie knew of only one Alan. It must be about tomorrow night's party, she thought. Perhaps the boys couldn't come. Had someone found out what they were all up to? Was there trouble ahead?

She raced up to the main hall.

"Alan?"

"Jennie?" The voice was a husky whisper.

"No, it's Rosie. I'll give her the message. She can't come to the phone right now. What is it? Is it about the party?"

"The party? No. It's not about any party. Listen, I've got to meet Jennie. It's urgent."

"Are you all right, Alan?"

"No, I'm not all right. I told you, it's urgent. Tell Jennie to meet me at half four on the dot at the corner of Dorset Street."

"Is there anything else? You sound strange."

"You'd sound strange too if you had to do stupid things like this. Just tell her. Half four pronto."

Before Rosie could say anything else, he hung up.

By the time she got back to the dinner table Jennie was there and she passed on the message. "He told Mother Misericordia he's your cousin," she added.

"Well, he had to," Jennie said. "Otherwise there'd be an inquisition. But cousin or not, the Head will have a fit if she thinks I'm meeting him. She'll wonder why he couldn't come to the school and she'll get very suspicious."

"Maybe he should come to the school, then."

Jennie thought about it, then shook her head. "No. Old Misery will insist on meeting him. He'll never manage to fool her and then we'll both be in trouble. I'll have to sneak out and hope no one notices. But we've early Study at four and if I'm missing there'll be uproar."

She discussed ways of escape with Rosie and Katie but they could think of no plan which wouldn't lead to calamity. Mother Misericordia was taking Study and any one absent without an excuse would be looking for disaster.

Rosie thought the situation was ridiculous. "I don't see why you can't say you're going out to meet your boyfriend. I mean, the world wouldn't collapse, would it?"

The other two were aghast. They opened and shut their mouths without a sound emerging. Finally Katie said, "No, it'd be worse than that. Much worse. It'd be Mother

121

Misericordia who'd collapse and – and – and –" Her words were tripping up with agitation. She took a deep breath and finished, "And Jennie would probably end up in solitary confinement, waiting to be collected by her parents."

"Well, I think the rules are insane," Rosie said.

"I think your suggestion is insane," Katie told her. "I hope you've no more mad ideas. You're no help."

The three were on their way to afternoon class when Stacia Bolger stopped them. "Thanks for the books," she said. "Mother Misericordia delivered them."

Jennie's eyes widened.

"Oh, I gave them to her," Rosie said vaguely, her mind still on the problem.

"Did you?" the senior smiled. "You had quite a little chat with her too. About sleeping in a dead girl's bed."

The other two, knowing nothing of the prefect's efforts to terrify Rosie with a ghost story, wondered now had the senior lost her mind altogether.

"So? Why wouldn't I mention that?" Then she remembered 2A wasn't talking to Stacia and added loftily, "What I talk about to Mother Misericordia is no concern of yours."

Katie and Jennie stared at her. What was going on? How had Rosie managed to get Mother Misericordia to deliver a sack of books for her. Why did they have a conversation about a dead girl's bed?

She's very brave, Jennie decided.

She's a total lunatic, Katie thought.

Stacia's smile vanished. With some effort it reappeared. "Anyway, it's not you I want to talk to, Rosie McGrath. It's Jennie. Your painting needs you in the Art room at four o'clock, Jennie, otherwise it will be an unfinished masterpiece. That's the message from Miss Madden."

The prefect walked away while Jennie moaned, "I can go to Study, I can go to the Art room but I can't get out of school."

"Yes, you can," Rosie said. "You can. Tell Old Misery the Art teacher wants you and tell Miss Madden you have Study. They'll each think you're with the other. It's perfect. You won't even have to lie."

"You're so clever," Jennie said.

"Total genius," Katie said, rapidly revising her previous opinion.

At four o'clock Jennie put the plan into action. It worked perfectly, though there could have been a hitch when Mother Misericordia asked, "That phone call – your cousin Alan – is everything all right?"

"Yes, Mother. It's just about some arrangements – arrangements to meet before Christmas. It's not really urgent."

"No, but it's nice when your parents are away to have family thinking of you. I suppose your cousins will want to see you before you go to New York?"

Mother Misericordia wasn't generally so understanding and Jennie felt guilty, but not for long. If she told the truth, the principal would turn back into the raging demon they were used to, so the girl smiled and nodded and disappeared as fast as possible.

Miss Madden made no difficulties, "Well, you're almost finished and on Friday morning you can put the last touches to the painting. I think until then I'll keep it at the back of the staff room which is next to the boiler room. The air is warm but not too hot and it should dry nicely. I'm glad you're taking a break, Jennie."

Swiftly Jennie got her coat and slipped out the back way. Looking around first, she sped across the nuns' garden, through the door in the high wall, and down the long lane towards Dorset Street. From a classroom on the first floor Stacia Bolger watched, keeping well back from the window until the second-year disappeared. She smiled at her own cleverness. Jennie had used the plan she, Stacia, had handed her on a plate with that message from Miss Madden.

The Art teacher had been a little surprised when Stacia told her the younger girl wanted to spend more time after school on the picture. "Tell her to come at four if she wants, though she might be better taking a break. It's good of you to consider her, Stacia." And puzzling too, she thought. Stacia didn't usually show much concern for others and Miss Madden had wondered at the Head's decision to make her a prefect. Well, perhaps the Head was right after all.

Stacia's picture was finished over a week ago: a portrait of her father, done in watercolours, now on an easel at the back of the Art room. Miss Madden knew John Bolger. He was a vain man, good at self-publicity. Stacia hadn't captured any of his character. The face she'd painted – although all the features required in a face were present –

124

was lacking in personality and character. Her picture was like a bland photo and in fact she had painted her father from a photo, wanting the end result to be a surprise for him. The leather armchair he sat in was perfectly executed, as was his desk, the table lamp and the bookshelves behind him. The props had more life than the man and because of this wonderfully precise background Miss Madden thought it had a chance of winning – until Jennie decided to enter.

Stacia's picture was safe on its easel. Jennie's she took away to dry. On Friday she would deliver both to the offices of the National Art Competition. It was nice the prefect could show such generosity of spirit towards her younger rival.

With anything but generosity, Stacia hurried into the Study Hall and made her way up to Mother Misericordia.

The loud whispers coming from the platform raised heads. In the second row, Rosie was dismayed by the disjointed words she heard: "*Jennie Bolger – meeting a boyfriend – telephone call – gone before I could stop her – not at Art, no. Positive, Mother.*" Stacia's hissing grew louder until finally the head nun was convinced.

Mother Misericordia rose from her desk and addressed the girls, "You are on your honour to continue with your work in silence until my return."

She swept out of the room, Stacia after her.

Five seconds later, Rosie followed.

The nun hurried to her quarters to get her overcoat while Stacia waited impatiently in the main hall. Not bothering with a coat, Rosie had a head start and took the back way, zooming across the lawn.

Down the long lane she raced until her heart was pounding. Her route was longer than Mother Misericordia's, but the nun wouldn't be as fast.

Running out onto Dorset Street, past all the old derelict houses, she spied Jennie at the corner of Eccles Street and stopped short at what she saw: a boy, a young man of nineteen or twenty was gripping the girl's arm, shouting at her to stay still.

"I'm not going to hurt you!" he was yelling. "As soon as your damn principal sees us, I'm off. So stop trying to get away, will you?"

Jennie struggled even more and the fellow gripped harder.

Rosie could see only one solution. She hurtled along Dorset Street and straight into the young man. Winded, he let go, staggered and fell. Open-mouthed Jennie looked down at him.

"Who the hell are you?" she said.

"Come on," Rosie seized her, "Old Misery is on her way with Stacia."

The two girls started running. Behind them the young man was struggling to his feet, shouting after them, "I'm going to kill Delia! Getting me involved in stupid games!"

At the turn into the lane Rosie glanced back.

Mother Misericordia and Stacia were at the corner. Catching sight of them, the young man hastened across the main road, eager to get far away.

Inside the back door of St Catherine's both girls stopped, leaning against the wall, breath heaving.

"Come on," Rosie said. "If we hurry we'll get there

before those two. You can't be expelled just because you were late for Study."

"I've no books," Jennie gasped.

"I'll give you some. Come on."

They made it with more than twenty minutes to spare because it didn't occur to Mother Misericordia that Jennie might be in the Study Hall. Instead the nun looked in the dormitory, in the gym and common room and anywhere else the girl might be hiding. Stacia was half satisfied. While her plan hadn't quite worked, it seemed Jennie O'Neill hadn't returned yet and would be in awful trouble when she did.

Worried now, the nun asked Mother Clementine to do a further search while she checked on her charges. She went back to the Study Hall hoping nothing bad had happened. Stacia was still in tow. Opening the door, the principal stopped in shock and the prefect ran into her.

"Why are you still following me?" the nun said. "I'll see you later. Leave this to me."

Reluctantly Stacia went, though not before she had seen Jennie O'Neill, head bent, studying away at a desk in the silent hall. The prefect's disappointment was immense.

When Old Misery tapped her shoulder, Jennie feigned surprise and jumped. "Follow me," the head mouthed.

No one looked around until they'd left, then a buzz of whispered questions erupted. Rosie shook her head, a finger on her lips signalling silence. She would tell them afterwards. A hush descended.

"Where have you been?"

Mother Misericordia looked fit to burst and Jennie mustered all her acting abilities.

"I've been in there, Mother, studying. What's wrong?"

"You were supposed to be in the Art room, Jennie. Now, once again, where were you?"

"I *was* in the Art room, Mother, talking to Miss Madden and she was saying I needed a break and to leave the painting until Friday. So I came to Study, instead." Jennie hoped she looked virtuous. "Sorry I was late," she added.

Mother Misericordia wasn't finished. "I shall of course check with Miss Madden. This phone call you got, it was from your cousin? Stacia Bolger seems to think a boyfriend was trying to contact you."

"That's not true, Mother!" The girl was genuinely indignant. "And I don't know why Stacia said so. There was no boyfriend trying to phone me."

Jennie swallowed, raging at the prefect.

The head nun narrowed her eyes and looked hard at the girl. Usually even the innocent found it hard to face the head's searching look, but Jennie was so furious nothing could daunt her and she glared into the nun's eyes.

The only reason for such anger, thought Mother Misericordia, was enraged innocence.

"Go back to Study, Jennie." The nun's voice was weary, "I'll deal with this later."

If the girl's story checked out, she thought grimly, Stacia Bolger would have to account for her actions.

Chapter 21

Jennie *was* raging. And she felt innocent. The phone call, the meeting with the stranger, Mother Misericordia turning up – these were all part of a plot to get her expelled. It didn't need much intelligence to know who was behind it and how it was engineered. It was obvious from the roars and shouts of the fellow that Delia was involved, which meant Stacia had planned it all, which was obvious anyway from the prefect's rush to tell Old Misery in the Study Hall.

Given the right information, a pigeon brain could work out who the culprits were. But Mother Misericordia didn't have that information. All she saw was a prefect doing her duty.

They had to do something, otherwise the sixth-year's schemes would grow more and more outlandish.

"How does she know about Alan?" Rosie said.

"It wouldn't be difficult," Katie answered. "She'd have seen him and Jennie at hockey. And we've met the lads a few Sundays. She must have noticed he was hanging around."

"She has to be stopped," Jennie said, "before she does something worse."

Rosie agreed, all too aware of the danger. According to the catalogue note of 2007, Jennie O'Neill had been expelled.

"But what else can she do?" Katie said. "She's done her worst . . . unless she destroys your painting!"

Katie frightened herself at the thought but Rosie, knowing the future, said, "No, she won't have the nerve to do that."

"Especially since it's in the staffroom now," Jennie said. "It'd be easier to get into Fort Knox."

The teachers of St Catherine's were famous for their refusal to let a student cross the door of the staffroom, no matter what the emergency.

"It's a child-free zone," Locky had once explained. "The only child-free area in the school. After all, how would you feel if teachers wandered into your common room?"

"Mother Misericordia wanders in all the time," they'd informed her, a little bitterly.

"Yes, but Mother Misericordia doesn't teach. She's not a teacher," Locky replied, as if that answered everything.

"Well, she's not a schoolgirl, unless she's disguised – really absolutely, heavily disguised," someone said.

After that the discussion soured and Locky gave them a lecture on sarcasm and cheek. But they'd got the message that if any student ever ventured into the staffroom she'd probably be hanged, or worse.

Jennie's painting was safe.

Stacia blamed Delia for the plan's failure.

"You're a complete eejit!" she told her new best friend. "You can't do anything right."

"Does this mean you're not letting me copy your exams?" Delia got straight to what was important.

Stacia wasn't finished. "And not only are you an eejit, but your brother is one too. You're a family of eejits!"

The new best friend was well aware of her own short-comings. Since she'd never passed an exam, it was difficult for anyone to see her as other than stupid, she knew that. Somewhere at the back of her mind though was the suspicion that exams didn't prove everything and that one day she would show people they were wrong.

Her brother, on the other hand, was a great passer-of-exams. Furthermore, Delia liked him. He was always standing up for her at home and she felt very mean at how she'd treated him. She'd never intended to carry out her blackmail threat, but he wasn't to know that and now he probably hated her.

At this stage Stacia was calling everyone belonging to her an eejit and Delia lost her temper.

"Shut up!" she said. "Just shut up about my brother! All he did was try to help. I've a good mind to tell Mother Misericordia what's going on."

Stacia shut up, but only for a second. "You'd just get yourself into trouble," she said then.

"I don't care. You're the one with the plans. I followed them perfectly and look how useless they were. You're the fool, Stacia, a big fool. It's about time Mother Misericordia found out what you're like."

Frightened by the girl's hysteria, Stacia was silent, thinking rapidly. Then she sighed and said, "You can't tell the Head because your brother will get into trouble too. Your parents won't like what he did." When she saw the realisation on Delia's face, she added, "You're right. You did follow the plans perfectly and it's not your fault at all that things went wrong. If Mother Misericordia hadn't delayed so much, she'd have seen Jennie O'Neill with your brother, but that wasn't your fault."

Delia calmed down and Stacia said sorry over and over till she thought the apologies might be overdone, but from the happier look on the girl's face she saw they had worked. Later she would think of another plan. It would have to be more drastic this time and it might be harder to convince Delia to carry it out. But she would convince her. She would also make sure to get her own story right because she'd no doubt now that if Delia was found out, she would tell everything.

And if she is caught, Stacia thought with some satisfaction, it will show her exactly who the fool is.

After tea, Rosie skipped going to the common room. There was something she needed to do far more than watch *Z Cars* on a flaky telly and some moments later she was at the door of the nuns' parlour asking for Mother Benedicta.

The nun was in her late twenties. She looked as if she never smiled although the kindness in her blue eyes softened her expression. When she saw Rosie, she started back slightly, then asked, "What can I do for you?"

"I was just wondering – do you know whether – well, the bed I'm sleeping in . . ." – Rosie did not want to be blunt and as a result was stumbling.

The nun said quietly, "You're in my sister Caroline's old bed. I know."

The worst over, Rosie forged ahead now. "Can you tell me if her ring was ever found? I read about it in *The Lanthorn*."

Mother Benedicta showed no surprise at her knowledge and said, "No, I'm afraid it wasn't. People gave up looking for it years ago, but I keep hoping. It would go now to my small niece, when she's old enough. Something of Caroline's for her to treasure."

She didn't ask why Rosie was so curious. She didn't ask anything. Yet when Rosie thanked her and was about to turn away, she said, "You remind me of Caroline. I've seen you on the corridors, full of fun and mischief. She was tall for her age too and had the same lively expression as you."

Not knowing what to say, Rosie nodded, and after a moment Mother Benedicta nodded too and closed the door.

It was time to search the storeroom properly and though she didn't believe in ghosts Rosie wasn't going in there again on her own. Any number of times she'd started to tell Jennie and Katie about the ghost story and Caroline Browne and *The Lanthorn* but always something important interrupted her. She would tell them tonight, she decided, and then the three of them would look for the ring.

Chapter 22

Rosie didn't see the others on their own again that evening. Supper was followed by a decade of the rosary and a lecture from Mother Misericordia on the "Behaviour Expected of St Catherine Girls During The Silent Retreat".

Having delivered half an hour's talk, Mother Misericordia put up a large notice in the common room.

Rules for the Retreat

- *The retreat will start at 7am and finish after evening chapel.*
- *There will be no talking. Failure to keep silent will merit punishment.*
- *There will be no communication apart from the exchange of holy pictures.*
- *Girls should not seek out each other's company, but stay on their own.*
- *There will be no eating between meals, which will be sparse in the true spirit of fasting and penance.*

- *The day should be spent in meditation, prayer and reading.*
- *The chapel will be open all day, as will the nuns' garden and the second-year common room.*
- *Religious reading material will be made available to you.*
- *Any questions for Father Hubert may be placed in the Question Box after first Mass and at any time during the day.*
- *Finally, I wish you all an excellent retreat.*

"It's a strictly no-fun time," Rosie muttered. "And we'll be starving. Not that the food is up to much anyway."

Mentally she listed her least favourite items on the St Catherine's menu: oxtail soup (unspeakable), steak and kidney pie with dumplings (greasy), tinned tongue (horrible) and grilled gammon steaks (tough as nails) with a slice of tinned pineapple on top.

For dessert she'd tried watery tinned fruit salad, tapioca, burnt semolina and bread pudding – all horrible. Angel Delight was nice, a bit like flavoured whipped cream. She especially liked the chocolate version. But in general the meals were awful. Hungrily she thought of the beautiful food in her rucksack, kept for the party. It would be worth the wait.

At bedtime she tried to talk to Jennie and Katie, but everyone in the dorm was around them, discussing Stacia's latest spite and then tomorrow night's party. The only thing to do, decided Rosie, was to set the alarm for the middle of the night and wake the other two. Nobody in the dormitory was allowed an alarm-clock, since Mother

Benedicta wanted sole charge of time, but on the skirting board right beside her bed Rosie had spied an electric socket. Now, unnoticed by the others, she took her mobile from the rucksack and put it on charge. She was relieved when it lit up. The Powers That Be were allowing her to use her mobile. Great! She fixed the alarm for 3am.

"*Meep-maaaaaaw, meep-maaaaaaw –*" The demented sound woke her on the dot. Swiftly she stopped the noise and sat up. No one else was disturbed. Silently she crept over to Jennie. Placing a hand over the girl's mouth she tugged and shook her till she woke. For a second Jennie's eyes widened with fear, then she nodded at Rosie's signal to be quiet.

Katie choked and gasped, but eventually realised it was Rosie and was silent. Rosie got her torch and, tiptoeing, they followed her down the corridor. She knew they wouldn't go into the storeroom without protest, so instead she led the way to the bathroom and told them everything she knew about Caroline Browne.

Their questions were slow and sleepy. Both of them had heard of Caroline Browne but they'd never heard of the sapphire ring. That such a treasure might be hidden in the school awakened their excitement, which took a steep dive when Rosie mentioned the storeroom.

"I don't believe in ghosts," Katie said, "but that room is creepy."

"I don't see why we have to search it at 3am," Jennie added. "It's not as eerie during the day, though it's bad enough. Why can't we do it then?"

"When, exactly?" Rosie asked. "Tomorrow we've got the retreat and I bet Mother Misericordia will be watching us like a hawk. Friday you've got to concentrate on your painting. Saturday – well, Saturday . . ."

Saturday she was going home.

"All right," Jennie understood. "We'll look now."

"I don't know what's wrong with Saturday," Katie grumbled, but she followed the others.

The room was intensely cold and hushed. The only sound tonight was their breathing which became more and more shallow.

"Keep your nerve," Rosie whispered.

The strong beam from her torch made it easier to see.

"I searched near the window," she whispered, "so we could start behind that old sofa."

They looked under crumbling newspapers, yellow and curling. They searched in the ancient desks and along the bookshelves. Their wits scattered and they almost shrieked when a dusty almanac fell with a clatter on the wooden floor. They looked everywhere – behind tattered cushions and even in the hollows of brass candlesticks. There was no ring.

Eventually they reached the door again and Rosie sighed, "I was sure we'd find it here. I mean, why else would she have been in here the night she caught pneumonia?"

"I don't know," Katie was very grumpy, "but if we stay here much longer, *we'll* catch pneumonia."

"How do you know she was in here? Was it in *The Lanthorn?*" Jennie asked.

"No. Stacia told me –" She stopped. Stacia's words and the truth could be two different things.

"Stacia?" snorted the other two. "You believed Stacia?"

With that they were out of the room and making their way to the dormitory, very cross indeed.

Before dawn the dormitory door opened and the pale figure moved across the room. For a few moments she stood by Rosie's bed and briefly touched the girl's forehead. Then she was gone.

Chapter 23

The school was unnaturally quiet on Thursday morning, not a word spoken on the way to the chapel at 7am. As Father Hubert said Mass and gave a long talk on the responsibilities of young womanhood, Rosie's mind slid away and slumbered.

At breakfast, Mother Clementine read a little homily while Rosie stared with dismay at the single slice of bread and butter on her plate. This was taking starvation to unnecessary lengths.

Afterwards holy pictures were on sale in the common room – the proceeds would go the missions – and Rosie was surprised that everyone bought them.

She hung back, having no money, but Jennie got a pack for her and they spent the next hour exchanging inscribed pictures with the rest of 2A.

Rosie tried to visualise her classmates in CCS collecting holy pictures. Her imagination failed.

By mid-morning the day was dragging. There seemed to be nuns on every corridor and in every nook and cranny.

Popping up to the dormitory for a snooze was impossible. Rosie visited the chapel three times for something to do.

There was the odd whisper as friends crossed paths on the corridors or the hint of nervous laughter when girls passed each other but really Rosie couldn't understand how most people were managing to stay silent.

The nuns' garden was bitterly cold and, although the day was bright, the frost was thick. After ten minutes of trudging around the flowerbeds Rosie's nose and fingers were numb and she went in again.

Once she passed Stacia Bolger and they ignored each other.

Wandering like a lost soul along the warren of corridors, she thought of Jennie. Over the next two days Jennie could be expelled. Something awful was going to happen, but what? Was it something to do with tonight? Was she, Rosie, going to be the cause of Jennie's expulsion? Perhaps a party with boys in a convent boarding school was a fairly stupid idea after all . . .

Turning a corner she saw Delia Waters coming towards her. The senior was in a daydream and didn't notice Rosie till she was almost beside her. She stopped short and Rosie waited for a smart comment but to her surprise the girl's face reddened and she looked away, looked back, nodded and rushed off. Rosie stared after her, wondering was she making too much of it to imagine that Delia seemed embarrassed and sorry.

With time to kill before dinner Rosie wandered back to the common room and picked up *The Story of Father Damien*. Soon she was engrossed in the horrors of leprosy;

in descriptions of fingers and toes falling off and dreadful things happening to noses and ears.

Nevertheless when the bell went Rosie raced to the refectory, starving and looking forward to something a bit more generous than breakfast.

Her disgruntlement was deep: another cup of tea and a single slice of buttered bread. How could anyone call this dinner? All around her a collective sigh of grief went up.

Dinner was over in less than three minutes.

Starving now, Rosie found the afternoon even longer than the morning. Chapel, common room, garden, common room, chapel, garden, round and round she went.

At evening chapel Father Hubert's sermon was about the Last Supper and Rosie dreamed of her favourite foods: fresh breads, glorious cheese, abundant grapes, lemon and lime juice, pizzas, meringues and cream, blueberry pie, apple tarts . . .

She was ravenous.

Six girls were invested as Children of Mary, none of them second-years and Rosie was relieved that neither Jennie nor Katie looked too disappointed.

Finally the priest read through a selection from the Question Box, most asking for prayers for special intentions. One asked if it was a sin for a girl to go out alone with a boy.

With one accord everyone turned around and looked at Mother Misericordia in the back row. This topic was dear to her heart and they all knew her views. Now someone was looking for a second opinion and every girl was curious to see the Head's reaction.

Mother Misericordia got very red and flustered and waved her hands at them to turn around at once.

Father Hubert answered the question briefly: "If a girl goes out with a boy, she is *not* alone and that's that."

The principal was furious with Father Hubert who, she decided, had deliberately misinterpreted the question and ruined her careful guidance. A typical man, she thought, he did not want to get involved with the difficulties of females.

The girls smiled in delight at the answer.

At last – at last – the retreat was over and talking was back on. Rosie's heart sang.

Chapter 24

"There's one thing we never thought of," Jennie said as they were getting ready for bed. "How are we going to wake up in time for the party? We've no alarm-clock."

"I've an alarm," Rosie said.

They stood waiting and reluctantly she took the charged mobile from her locker. Mesmerised, they watched her finger work the keyboard and set the alarm.

"What is that?" Katie breathed.

"Is it a miniature typewriter?" Jennie asked.

"I've never seen anything like it," Katie frowned. "Never. Where did you get it?"

"It's Japanese," Rosie told her.

"Who cares where she got it?" Jennie tried to sound indifferent though she couldn't stop staring at the mobile. "We've other things to sort out."

Food was one of them. Since Sunday 2A had hoarded sweets and chocolates from the tuck shop and now everyone put their purchases on Jennie's bed. Rosie made her

143

contribution and they were amazed. No one had seen cans of Coke before. The openers fascinated them even more than the cans. The variety of food was exotic to their eyes. "*Chocolate Kimberly*," one girl read, "*Pure Heaven*." They examined the six kinds of crisps, the giant pack of popcorn, the chocolate mallows and the monster fruit chews with reverence. Flake bars they'd seen before, but then someone noticed '*praline*' on the wrapper and Rosie had to explain that praline gave the most delicious crunch and taste to the chocolate.

It had been a long hungry day and they looked at the Rosie's stash with solemn adoration. "You must have got all this on the continent." Someone lifted a jar and studied it, "What does shimmer taste like? It sounds delicious."

"Sorry, that's make-up," Rosie said. She extracted some tubes and cylinders and flat boxes. "Mascara, blusher, cream, eye-shadow and lip-gloss."

"Wow!"

If possible, the make-up drew even more veneration than the food and they handled each item in turn, passing it on like a precious object.

"Right," Jennie said, "we can't stand staring. All this has to go into the press. I sneaked up the turntable earlier and we'd better sort out what singles we want to play. When Stacia gets here everything has to look normal."

When Stacia arrived everything was so normal the prefect was instantly suspicious. Yesterday no one in 2A would speak to her. Now they talked to her as though nothing had happened. Even Jennie O'Neill and her friends weren't hostile. What was going on?

Stacia delayed. She walked up and down the dormitory after they were all in bed. Nothing was out of place. She crossed over to Rosie. The girl's eyes were closed though the prefect was certain she wasn't asleep.

"Put the lights out, Stacia!" someone called. "We're jaded after the retreat."

Maybe that was it, she thought. They'd decided to be nicer because of the retreat.

Suspicions fading, Stacia switched off the light and left.

At eleven thirty Rosie's alarm went and after a few minutes girls were sitting up in bed. Lights on, a military operation went into effect. The two rows of beds and the lockers were lifted back to give more space in the middle of the room.

All sweets and drinks were divided between the first three beds. The turntable was set up on Rosie's locker, near the socket. The make-up was taken to the bathroom and it was then control gave way to great excitement. Everyone had to try everything and they thought the results were magnificent:

"My eyes are fab with that bronze stuff!"

"Look at my lips!"

"That shimmer is beautiful!"

Their voices grew higher with each new effect.

"Shut up!" Rosie said, but no one heard her. "Shut up! You'll wake everyone!" They paid no attention and in desperation she roared, "*Shut up!*"

There was an instant hush. They listened for any sound of disturbance, looking reproachfully at Rosie. Between them they had used every bit of make-up and she was handed the empty containers. The make-up had cost her a fortune and it would be ages before she could replace it all. Did they have to use it all? It was so annoying.

Back in the dormitory Katie came over, "I haven't changed my mind about you, you know. There is something strange about you."

The girl was wearing Rosie's blusher, her mascara, her shimmer and her lip-gloss and had some nerve starting all this again.

Rosie was about to snap when Katie added, "But you're really generous. That make-up is fab. You must have spent all your pocket money on it and you've given it all to us. That's decent." She smiled and Rosie smiled back.

Five minutes later Jennie was unlocking the back door with the great iron key from the hook nearby. Light snow was falling and an outdoor lamp made a pool of light around the seven boys. They were freezing, overcoat collars pulled up, pyjama legs stuffed into socks or, in Jimmy's case, tooled leather cowboy boots with sharp pointed toes.

They didn't speak. Once inside they took off their footwear and left them by the door. They crept up the stairs after Jennie and without mishap reached 2A's dormitory.

"Fab! This is fab!" Jimmy's admiration had no bounds as he surveyed the scene. Tinsel and balloons draped the lockers and bedsteads. On the front of each wardrobe was a colourful poster proclaiming *MERRY CHRISTMAS*.

Someone put on the single, 'Rock around the Clock.'

"Too square," Katie said and substituted 'All my Lovin'.'

The girls threw pillows onto the floor and as soon as everyone got some food and drink they sat around in a circle. The talk was subdued at first, the atmosphere a little tense. After all this was the worst thing they had ever done in their lives and if anybody in authority ever found out they'd be expelled. That thought made them very solemn, but only for a short while. As they ate and drank and talked and listened to the music they gradually relaxed.

"Party time!" Jimmy jumped up. He'd brought a Rolling Stones LP and as soon as the first number started he was over to Rosie. "Dance?" he said.

Soon the pillows were back on the bed and everyone was dancing. Rosie was bemused. Jimmy was doing some sort of snake step, twisting lower and lower, so that his body disappeared. Throwing his feet out, he looked like a head on legs.

How is that possible? Rosie thought.

Someone raised the sound and as the rhythm took hold they forgot school for a while.

Chapter 25

On the second floor in the sixth-year dormitory, Delia Waters couldn't sleep because she couldn't stop thinking: about exams, about her brother, about the rotten trick with Jennie O'Neill's copy and the even worse plan to get her caught with her 'boyfriend'.

Delia wasn't doing Art for the Leaving and she wondered now what Jennie's painting was like. It must be wonderful to be able to paint well. To do anything at all well must be nice, she mused wistfully. She'd gone to such trouble to get the second-year out of the competition, yet she didn't even know what her picture was like. She hadn't even seen Stacia's work, though the girl had given her a glowing description. Surely she should at least look at both pictures, since she'd plotted so much for one of them to win. She should go down to the Art room and she should go now when there was no one there to say she was intruding.

Delia tossed and turned and the idea tossed and turned with her. It wouldn't let her alone and finally she got up, put on her slippers and left the dormitory.

A few beds away, Stacia, also awake, thought the girl was on her way to the bathroom.

As Delia turned on the second landing she imagined for a mad moment that she could hear music high above her. Was it the Stones? No, it had to be her imagination. The stairs creaked on her way down. Afraid to put on the light, Delia focussed on each step and wished it wasn't so dark. The walls seemed to loom in on her. Down the corridor she saw a small red glow and almost turned back, until she realised it was a night light in front of the statue of Saint Dominic. Gratefully she took the small candle from its red glass and made her way to the Art room.

No one would see a light on in here, she thought, but when she flicked the switch the bulb was gone. Working her way around by candlelight, Delia saw many pictures but didn't think any of them was Jennie's.

She recognised the portrait of Mr Bolger from Stacia's description. Holding the candle close, she thought how talented it was, just like a photograph, though Mr Bolger's face looked a little blank. But the books and shelves and all the furnishings were exact and Delia was impressed.

On her way back to the door she bumped into the edge of a table and, stumbling slightly, she righted herself but not quickly enough. The candle fell onto some sketches and a flicker caught the corner of a page. Delia looked around for something to douse the rising flame. The sink was much further away than a damp cloth on a nearby easel. She threw the cloth on the small fire, but it was moist with white spirit and blazed.

Soon the flames spread across the table and Delia panicked. The room was full of paints and spirits and might well become an inferno. She ran to the door.

Then pausing, she thought: Stacia's painting! I've got to get it. She'll kill me if I don't! She raced back to the top of the room and grabbed the watercolour. By the time she reached the door again, her eyes were streaming and she was finding it hard to breathe. Fervently she hoped Jennie's painting wasn't in there.

When Delia didn't come back from the bathroom, Stacia, wide awake, decided to look for her. On the second landing she too heard music, and she didn't think it was her imagination. It was coming from upstairs, way upstairs. It was coming from 2A's dormitory and she raced upwards.

Stacia got the shock of her life when she opened the dormitory door. It was a scene from a strange dream: boys and girls in pyjamas rocking away to the Rolling Stones; balloons and tinsel; cans of drink.

She couldn't be awake. She *was* awake. "What's going on?" she shouted but no one heard. She was going to flick off and on the light for attention when the element of surprise occurred to her. If Mother Misericordia saw this . . .

Stacia turned on her heel just as Jimmy spotted her.

"There was someone racing away," he told Rosie. "A girl, a bit older than us."

Rosie turned and saw the open door and had a really bad, sinking feeling. "We're in trouble," she said.

Jimmy was across to the record player in no time and when the music stopped so did the dancing.

"I think Stacia saw us," Rosie told them.

The prefect had reached the nun's quarters when she had second thoughts about waking Mother Misericordia. She wasn't the head's favourite person just now and she could imagine the nun's face puckering with sourness when she saw her.

It was then Stacia had her brainwave.

In a few seconds she was at the fire alarm, smashing the glass with the hammer alongside. The noise nearly deafened her. Holding her ears she rushed back to her dormitory, almost colliding with Delia Waters who was carrying her painting.

"What are you doing with my picture?" she said.

"You set off the alarm. How did you know there was a fire in the Art room?" Delia said, shoving the watercolour under her bed, just as everyone else in the dormitory began to wake.

"What? Never mind, I'll talk to you later," Stacia told her. Then she took command. "Everyone, out of the dormitory! You know the fire drill. Down to the nuns' garden as quickly as possible."

Because of the possible danger everyone followed the drill. There was no exit by the front until one of the nuns unbolted and unlocked the heavy door. Safety was out the back way.

Stacia shivered with anticipation and imagined the scene about to unfold. The boys, trooping down from the upper storey just about now, must be quaking. They were nicely trapped. The headmaster of Ivor's would be summoned, parents called, scandal would follow, recriminations, expulsions, disgrace for everyone at that party . . . including Jennie O'Neill.

At ground-floor level, the air was thick and they could smell the smoke. The prefect remembered Delia's words and turned to her. "You said there was a fire in the Art room," she whispered. "What happened?"

Delia looked at her with hostility. "Don't worry," she muttered. "I got your picture out, didn't I?"

My God, Stacia thought, she set fire to the Art room! She looked at Delia with awe. "So Jennie O'Neill's painting is destroyed?"

Delia shrugged. "Every painting in there except yours must be ruined."

Stacia would have hugged her, but Delia had forced her way a couple of steps ahead.

Then suddenly it occurred to the prefect that she herself was a heroine. She had set off the alarm which was probably going to save lives. Mother Misericordia was bound to praise her quick thinking, possibly give her some award. Her father would be so proud. And now her painting had an excellent chance of winning the competition. On top of all that, a huge drama was just about to play out.

The future was glorious and Stacia hugged herself in anticipation.

Chapter 26

As soon as 2A thought Stacia had seen them, they had panicked. For one long minute the girls wrung hands, paced up and down and wailed. The boys were stunned into silence, looking at each other in consternation.

All except Jimmy.

"Shut up, everyone!" he yelled and ran around tugging and shaking people till they calmed down. Jumping onto a bed so that he could see everyone, he said forcefully, "It's only a party. It's not a crime. We can't lose control."

"He's right," Rosie said. "If the boys go immediately they might just make it before Mother Misericordia arrives. I'll bring them down to the back door. The rest of you could clear up here and throw everything into the wardrobes. With a bit of luck when Old Misery arrives we'll all be in bed. Come on, let's go. Come on, lads, hurry!"

If she was caught, Rosie thought, and didn't make it back to the dorm before the Head, well, she was only a visitor and she'd be gone on Saturday.

The boys grabbed their coats and flew out the door

behind her. They were down two flights when the fire alarm went. The noise made them move even faster and they paid no attention to the whiff of smoke drifting along the ground-floor corridor but hurtled down to the basement.

While Rosie opened the door they slipped on their shoes. Jimmy's foot was caught halfway down one of his cowboy boots and he cursed. In the end he gave up trying to force it and rushed out the door after the others, one boot swinging.

Then he turned back. "Rosie," he said, "no matter what, the party was a great idea. You're a genius." Rosie waved at him to move, but still he paused. "We're allowed take phone calls on Fridays between seven and eight. Will you ring me?"

"If I can," Rosie said. "Go on, Jimmy, please! I can hear people clattering down the stairs."

He was the only one in the garden now and the others were calling to him from beyond the wall. Still he stayed. "Promise you'll ring. Say you're my cousin. Phone calls are allowed from girls who are cousins."

"I promise," she said, and he was off, hobbling as fast as he could across the lawn. As the crowd came clattering down the last steps, he was over the wall. Rosie allowed herself to be swept into the garden and all the boys' snowy footprints were tramped on and lost as the school emerged to safety.

The drama that unfolded wasn't from Stacia's script. As the girls came out they followed the well-practised drill and got into line with their class. Some had managed to grab a coat or a jumper and most were wearing shoes, but all of them were freezing.

The nuns arrived and silence descended. Stacia waited and waited, her eyes focussed on the door. No boy emerged. Mother Clementine took a roll-call and ticked each name and still Stacia waited.

Now on the ground floor they could see the flames in the Art room. Where were the boys? Stacia grew afraid. Surely they weren't desperate enough to stay in a burning building, risking death. She slipped from her line across to 2A. Panicking, she said, "You can't leave them in there. They could die."

Katie answered, "Don't know what you're talking about."

"The boys, the boys at your party, the fellows from Ivor's. You can't leave them in there."

Taking pity on the prefect's hysteria, Katie said, "Calm down. There's no one in there."

"I saw them!" Stacia's voice rose. "They were in your dormitory. They should be here, safe."

"Listen," Katie seized the senior's arm and shook her. "Listen carefully: there's no one in there. All right? No one. Everyone got out."

It took Stacia some moments to understand, then she shook off Katie's hand and returned to her own class, seething with frustration.

In later years everyone remembered the excitement of that night; Mother Misericordia had rung the fire brigade and a lorry managed to get up the back lane. Firemen brought ladders into the garden. The Art-room window was broken and hoses were trained on the blaze. In the commotion the fierce cold was forgotten and there was much disappointment when, as soon as the flames were under control, an officer said they were to go back inside and stay in the basement area for the moment. It took another half hour to make the Art room safe and ensure nothing was left smouldering.

Then it was all over. Mother Misericordia said there would be an investigation next day into how the fire started, but for now they were to go back to their dormitories and tomorrow they could have an extra hour's sleep.

"Is everything in the Art room destroyed?" Stacia asked her.

"Everything. What the flames didn't burn the water ruined."

Jennie O' Neill might have got away with the party, Stacia thought, but her painting was gone. One way or another, the girl wouldn't be in that competition now, which was all that mattered.

Everyone slept. It seemed even St Catherine's ghostly figure was too exhausted to wander.

Chapter 27

Mother Misericordia called a general assembly next morning and informed the school that fire officers would be in the Art room all morning investigating the scene. "If anyone of you knows how it started, please come forward. It could save a lot of time." When no one said a word she continued, "There is at least one person here who knows something. I would appreciate it if the girl who set off the fire alarm would identify herself."

Stacia was tempted. She could step forward and say she smelled smoke and raised the alarm. She would be the heroine, honoured as such. Reluctantly she let the grand notion fade.

As soon as she woke that morning it had dawned on Stacia that the fire left her with major problems: everyone was bound to think it strange that hers was the only painting to escape the flames. Mother Misericordia was more likely to regard her as an arsonist than a saviour and to think her jealousy of Jennie O'Neill was the motive.

She looked at Delia's face. Of course she could point to her, but then Delia would confess everything.

The principal sighed. "The investigating officers will finish their work by lunch-time. I hope before then that anyone with any knowledge will come forward. If you volunteer information, you will be dealt with more leniently."

A short time later Stacia cornered Delia, "You'd better get my painting into that competition. The fire was your idea, so this is your problem. Make sure no one thinks I was involved."

"What do you think I should do?"

Stacia shrugged. "I haven't a clue, but you'd better manage it, otherwise you won't be cogging any of my tests."

Delia thought for a moment, then came to a decision. "I'll sort it out," she said. "You won't be involved and, by the way, the fire was an accident."

Stacia's smile was disbelieving.

"I don't care what you think," the other girl told her. "And I won't be cogging your exams. That was the worst idea ever and I'm sorry I thought about it for even a second. But I will sort this out and you won't be blamed, I promise." She left Stacia staring after her.

Soon afterwards the prefect got another shock.

Coming towards her down the corridor was the second-year trio she detested.

None of them could believe they'd got away with the party. If Mother Misericordia knew anything about it, had any proof, she'd have said so at assembly. Even if the whole school had gone on fire she'd have tackled them. Old Misery wouldn't let such a major crime pass without mention. So she must know nothing and now it was too late for any proof. The turntable was back in the common room before breakfast, the records packed away and everything else dumped into various bins around the school. They were safe and almost hysterical with relief.

Stacia couldn't bear their laughter and chat. Why was it they were so happy when everything was going wrong for her? She heard the word "party" and was infuriated.

"You got away with it," she said loudly.

Till then they hadn't noticed her. Now they stopped and smiled.

"I don't know why you're so cheerful, Jennie O'Neill. Maybe there's something you haven't realised?"

"Like what?" In spite of the fire this was a good day and Jennie couldn't be in bad form, even with Stacia.

"Like your painting being burned to a little heap of ashes in the Art room."

She said the words with relish.

Jennie shook her head. "But that didn't happen. Miss Madden took my picture out of there on Wednesday after school. She said it would dry better in the staffroom."

Shocked into breathlessness, the prefect could say nothing. The three girls stepped by her and continued down the corridor.

When they were out of earshot, Jennie said, "Oh God, I've just realised I can't finish my painting. What am I going to do?"

"Why not?" The other two were full of concern.

"The fire destroyed everything. I've no oil paints and I need them to finish it properly!" She was wailing now.

"Miss Madden could go and buy some," Katie suggested.

"Yes, but that could take an hour. It has to be left in by lunch-time. It's too much of a rush. I'll never do it."

"You will," Rosie said. "I have oil paints and a brush in my rucksack." As Katie turned astonished, she added, "Don't ask and don't say I'm strange. I'll get the oils, Jennie. Meet you at the staffroom."

And so it happened that Jennie was the only St Catherine's schoolgirl ever to set foot in the staffroom and spend a couple of hours there. Miss Madden rigged up a makeshift easel from a stack of books at the back of the room and the girl set to work, giving much thought to the tiny, final details, so absorbed she didn't hear teachers coming or going or a word of what they said – much to 2A's later disappointment.

Some time later, Delia was at the staffroom door handing Stacia's picture to Art teacher. Miss Madden's initial delight turned to puzzlement. "Why wasn't it destroyed? How is it here? What happened?"

Carefully Delia said, "Last night I couldn't sleep and I went down to the Art room to look at the paintings. I wanted to see Delia's and Jennie O'Neill's. I had a candle and it fell on some sketches. That's how the fire started, Miss. I rescued Stacia's picture because . . . well, because I thought she was my friend and I swear, I would have rescued Jennie's too but I couldn't see anything that was good enough to be hers."

It clicked with Miss Madden that the girl no longer

thought of the prefect as her friend. "Is Stacia putting pressure on you?"

"No, Miss, I don't want anyone to think Stacia is involved."

Miss Madden wondered. For now all she said was, "Luckily Jennie's painting is safe." The girl looked a lot happier at the news, Miss Madden noted. After some thought she said, "You've devastated my Art room, Delia, and that's a catastrophe, but it takes courage to own up, knowing all the trouble you're in. I admire that."

Delia smiled. She felt relief rather than dread. It was almost over, she thought, not just the last few days, but the last few years. With the crisis had come the realisation that she didn't want to live like this any more, always worried about her parents' disappointment, always hoping she'd pass the exams yet knowing she wouldn't. It was strange but this 'catastrophe' was a chance to get everything out in the open.

Miss Madden went with her to the Head's office. Mother Misericordia sat grim-faced as the girl told her story again and when she'd finished the nun said, "The Art room and everything in it is destroyed: all the paints, watercolours, materials, easels, all the tables and chairs. And all the students who study Art will be deprived of their room for the foreseeable future. It's a costly accident, Delia."

Miss Madden said something about insurance covering all the damage and the Head wondered at her sympathy.

Sharply, Mother Misericordia said, "We can't take this lightly. Expulsion is very much a possibility. Your parents will be summoned as soon as possible."

Delia was calm. "Yes, I think that's a good idea, Mother. They could come this evening. There are a few things to sort out with them. I don't mind at all being expelled, Mother. I'm useless at school and I'm not going to get my Leaving Cert and, even if you don't expel me, I won't be back next term. I'm fed up feeling stupid."

Delia had never said so many words to anyone in authority. Mother Misericordia stared at her. "But you're not stupid, Delia."

"I know that, Mother. But I panic before tests and everything I've learned slides out of my head."

Mother Misericordia forgot about expulsion. "Delia, Delia, you should have said so long ago. It may not be too late, you know. You can overcome your fear of exams with some help."

"Thank you Mother, but I'm not interested any more. Not everybody needs exams and I won't be doing any more of them."

Miss Madden admired the girl's politeness and composure. When Delia found courage, the teacher thought, she found it in abundance.

The Head too was impressed and wondered why she'd ever considered her dull. She should have made it her business to draw Delia out, to know about her. Now it was too late. "When your parents come in, we'll talk about this some more."

"Yes, Mother," Delia said. "We will. I don't want to go back to class, if that's all right."

"You can spend the day in the sixth-year common room. It won't be in use till tonight. I'll arrange for Ellen to bring your meals up. You may read, listen to music, look at television."

Miss Madden stared at the Head with wonder. Never had a culprit been treated with such niceness, especially someone who'd destroyed the Art room, caused the fire brigade to be summoned and the whole school to be evacuated in the early hours.

When Delia left the office the teacher hesitated, then said, "I've no proof, Mother, but I've a suspicion Stacia Bolger is involved in some way."

The principal sighed, "I've always prided myself on knowing my students. Now it turns out I don't know two of them at all."

When Delia didn't come back to class, Stacia grew more and more agitated. Unable to concentrate on lessons, she asked herself the same questions over and over. What was the girl doing? Had she gone to Miss Madden? What had she said? Something was very wrong.

It was nearly noon when she was summoned to the office.

Mother Misericordia's methods of interrogation were based on long years of experience and on one principle: take the suspect by surprise. She wasted no time, her sombre manner suited to a criminal investigation.

"Sit down, Stacia."

The prefect sat opposite and swallowed nervously as the Head stared at her silently, searching her soul so that whatever story the prefect had planned for this emergency evaporated instantly.

"Delia Waters has told me everything," she said at last, her voice hushed. Then, in spite of all her years as principal, she was shocked at the torrent of confession this unleashed.

It all came out: Jennie O'Neill's English copy; the phone call supposed to be from Jennie's boyfriend; setting off the fire alarm because of the party she'd seen in 2A's dorm; her great wish to get Jennie expelled and why; all about her father and his expectations and how he was such a great man and how all Stacia ever wanted was for him to be proud of her . . .

Mother Misericordia gave orders that no one was to disturb her in the office. Mother Clementine could deal with the fire-officers when they were finished and Mother Benedicta could cope with other school matters.

Then she gave all her attention to Stacia, listening, teasing out the problems, patient as the girl wept and sobbed and spilt every bean.

Then Stacia listened as the Head told her what would happen.

There would be no expulsion – that would do no good. In return, Stacia would say nothing ever about the midnight party. Mother Misericordia wanted no scandal and was certain 2A wouldn't breathe a word, knowing they'd be courting disaster.

It was essential, the Head said, that Stacia should see how well or badly she did in a straight competition, so her painting would not be withdrawn. However, the girl couldn't continue as prefect. That was her one punishment.

Aware that she was lucky Stacia agreed to the terms.

The principal added another: both parents must come in on Sunday for a meeting which Stacia would attend.

Mother Misericordia offered advice: "I want you to consider what you did and why you did it, especially why. Examine your actions, Stacia. Decide what kind of life *you* want."

The sixth-year was excused class and allowed instead to stay in the sick-bay until Sunday. It was a quiet place, suitable, the Head considered, for reflection. She wished she herself could go somewhere similar, but she had a school to run and duty called.

Chapter 28

Unaware of drama elsewhere, Rosie's last full day in St Catherine's passed peacefully. In English class Locky gave back her essay with a good mark, commenting on her "lively imagination". Then she asked each person to recite Gray's 'Elegy'. Rosie managed ten verses and was proud of the achievement. Katie and two others managed the whole poem and Locky handed over ten shillings. Satisfied enough with the all-round improvement the teacher gave no punishments. In fact she let them off homework and allowed ten minutes at the end to read a A Christmas Carol. Once she got home, Rosie determined, this was a book she would finish.

Jennie was in the refectory at lunch-time, back into the school routine. Her painting and Stacia's were by now safely delivered. Conversation was full of the midnight party and 2A waited for the prefect to march in and say something.

"I bet she's told Old Misery," Katie said.

"She's bound to," someone else said gloomily.

166

But the prefect never arrived, nor did Delia. A rumour started that both girls were sick, that they'd caught flu in the freezing garden during the fire. When someone mentioned the party again, Jennie said, "I don't think we should talk about it. If Mother Misericordia knew anything, we wouldn't be sitting here; we'd be expelled. So we'd better shut up and say nothing."

So they swore to silence. Yet in future years, until St Catherine's closed, the myth grew of a fabulous mixed party that a group of second-years once had, under the very nose of the strictest head-nun in history.

After school, Rosie saw Mother Benedicta and remembered some unfinished business.

"Can I help you, Rosie? Is there something you want?" She asked.

"Mother, I was wondering about your sister, Caroline. Did she spend a night in that old storeroom beside our dorm? Is that how she got sick? Was that where she was found?"

"Caroline was always delicate. That's why she got sick, and no, she wasn't found in the storeroom. She just couldn't get up one day. She was too ill."

The nun looked sad and Rosie was half-sorry she'd asked. Now at least she knew for certain that part of Stacia's story was untrue.

When she said as much to Jennie later, the girl said, "Another thing she lied about is those initials *CB* on your bedpost. Last night we were hiding stuff under mattresses and I saw something. Come on, I'll show you."

In the dormitory Jennie lifted up a mattress and showed

Rosie the same initials. Again, on the next bedstead the letters appeared and on the next. "One more thing I want to show you," Jennie said. "Let's lift the mattress off your bed."

Together they heaved mattress and bedclothes off and set them down on the floor. "Look there, at the top in the middle." Rosie had to get down on her knees to study the small script etched into the iron: *Chatham Beds*, she read.

"So this might not be Caroline's bed at all," she said.

"The same thing is on them all," Jennie told her.

Yet Mother Benedicta thought this was her sister's bed, Rosie mused. Well, there was no proof now. She was just about to stand up when a gleam caught her eye. Something was caught in the coiled iron mesh underneath the letters. She could not see clearly until she prised the metal strands away from each other. There, caught inside the spring was the sapphire ring. She stood up, the ring in her open palm.

"It's beautiful!" Jennie was awed.

Even in the winter light the gems winked.

Rosie closed her hand. "Let's give it to Mother Benedicta."

The nun was overcome. She gazed at Rosie with mute gratitude until the girl felt so awkward she started blushing and shifting from one foot to the other. At last Mother Benedicta said, "This means so much – not for the value because it will never be sold – but because it's connected to Caroline. I wonder how it came to be there?"

"Perhaps she put it under her pillow and it slipped down," Rosie said, "and no one would have seen it unless the mattress was lifted. Even then it mightn't have been noticed."

Again and again the nun thanked her. She couldn't thank her enough, and Jennie too.

Both girls heaved a sigh of relief when they finally got away.

"Mortifying," Jennie said.

"So embarrassing," Rosie agreed.

After tea Rosie thought of Jimmy. She had promised to ring him but there was no way she wanted to use the public phone in the hall. One bad experience with that was enough. Besides she'd have to ask for permission and give explanations and she wasn't going through all that. She'd have to get Ivor's on her mobile or not ring at all. She just hoped The Powers That Be would co-operate and allow her to use her mobile again.

Jennie gave her the phone number and at 7o'clock she managed to sneak out of the common room and up to the dormitory.

She dialled and it rang. It was working, thank goodness. In the long pause before the phone started ringing at the other end, she knew she'd miss Jimmy when she left.

"Hello. Is that you, Rosie?"

To her surprise, it was Jimmy. He had been waiting at the other end.

"It's me."

"Good."

There was a silence as both wondered what to say next. Jimmy took the plunge, "I was hanging around here,

169

hoping none of the priests would notice, so as soon as you rang I lifted the phone."

"Right."

"That's awful stupid, isn't it, because you know I lifted the phone, man, otherwise who are you talking to? You know what I mean?"

"I think so."

"I'm glad, because I don't."

They both laughed and the awkwardness was gone.

"That was fab last night, Rosie. Pure magic. Will you meet me on Sunday?"

There was such eagerness in his voice that she was almost tempted. Reluctantly she said, "I can't. Tomorrow I'm going home."

"Aw, Rosie. When will I see you again?"

"I don't know, Jimmy."

"Tell you what – I'll write to you at Quinos. Promise you'll write back."

"I'll answer any letter I get," She felt mean, especially when he cheered up immediately.

For a few more minutes they chatted and when he put down the phone Rosie sat on her bed, lost in sadness.

Hearing a noise she looked up and blinked in the poor light. Framed in the doorway was a figure she'd seen before, pale and ghostly. Before she could scream Mother Benedicta said, "I looked for you in the common room and was told you came up here."

Smoothing the skirt of her cream habit the nun crossed the room gracefully and almost silently.

"I wanted to give you this," she said. "It's just a thank

you for finding the ring and bringing it to me." Sitting on the bed beside her, the nun held out a box. In it lay a silver butterfly brooch and a delicate bracelet. I want you to choose one for yourself and give the other to Jennie. They were mine when I was your age.

"They're lovely," Rosie said. "Thank you!"

The nun stood up and nodded. Then she looked around the dorm. "I never sleep much at this time of the year. I think too much about Caroline and it makes me restless. Always I have to get up and walk around. She was so young and her death has haunted me. You've been very kind, Rosie, asking about her, and it's time I laid her ghost to rest. Getting back that ring has helped." For the first time she smiled.

I knew I was right, Rosie thought. Ghosts don't exist.

Chapter 29

Half an hour later Mother Misericordia came into the second-year common room. "I have some good news," she said, looking directly at Rosie. "Saint Aquinas College has received an all-clear from the Health Authorities. Though some girls are still recovering, there is no longer any danger of infection and you will be returning to the college at eleven in the morning."

Everyone in 2A crowded around, sad that she was going.

"You're good fun and I wish you could stay longer," Katie said, smiling, "Then maybe I could figure out why you're so different."

When the rest of the class trooped off to bed Rosie lingered with Jennie.

"I won't forget your letter," Jennie said. "The first thing I'll do, when I get to New York, is give it to my father."

"And you'll come to Gran's party too?" Rosie said.

Jennie smiled. "Of course I will, if I'm able." She paused, then said, "This was a wonderful week, Rosie. If it weren't for you I'd be expelled by now and my painting wouldn't be finished. And we'd never have had that party."

Rosie nodded, happy she'd come back, but sorry too. The next time they saw each other, Jennie would be in her fifties, sensible, settled and middle-aged, not at all like the girl who stood before her.

The events of the week suddenly exhausted them both and they could think no more. They made their way to bed, heads down.

Delia Waters emerged from the Head's office with her parents and saw them climbing the stairs. She might have called after Jennie but the Head was already opening the front door. Anyway, nothing she could say would change things. Delia looked around one last time. Then she ushered out her silent parents.

Next morning Mother Misericordia held another assembly. Briefly she mentioned the Art room and said the officers had done their work and it turned out the fire was accidental. She gave no details and changed the topic immediately.

"Today we say goodbye to the girls of St Aquinas College. We hope you've felt welcome and I shall be telling Mother Elisabeth that you've been the perfect guests." A cheer went up from different parts of the assembly and Mother Misericordia smiled before continuing, "Your school is expecting you back for lunch, so I want everyone packed and ready at the main door by a quarter to eleven. And all of us in St Catherine's wish you a very Happy Christmas."

This time everyone cheered their good wishes. The holidays were less than a week away. Freedom and Christmas beckoned.

When the buses came Mother Misericordia bustled, ticking names, hurrying up the girls. Rosie said her goodbyes again. Some of the girls from Quinos looked at her oddly on the bus, but they were busy waving out at their new-found friends or chatting about home or loading bags and their focus on Rosie was brief.

Looking out from a window seat at Mother Misericordia's flustered face, Rosie thought, Ellen was right. Old Misery isn't that bad. She had asked for the maid that morning, but it was Ellen's Saturday off. She left a thank-you note with Jennie.

Now, as soon as the buses were full, Mother Misericordia ushered the St Catherine girls up the steps. Each of 2A turned at the door, "Goodbye, Rosie!" they shouted. As she waved back the Head hustled them inside, giving out about their unseemly and unsuitable roars. Young ladies they were not.

The last girl in was Jennie, ducking and weaving behind the nun and yelling, "Bye, Rosie! See you in the next century!"

Mother Misericordia tut-tutted. "Most rude, Jennie. I thought you liked that girl. See you in the next century indeed. Not nice."

Jennie smiled and kept her secret.

As soon as the huge door closed, Rosie slipped out of her seat. "I forgot something," she said to the driver. "Don't wait, I'll get the other bus." She grabbed her rucksack and got off.

"She forgot everything, I'd say," someone said. "Did you see her knapsack? It's empty. Who is she anyway?"

"I thought she was from Catherine's."

"Well, she can't be, can she?"

No one knew. The topic intrigued them as the driver pulled away and they discussed it for a few more minutes. Then they forgot about Rosie in the excitement of going home.

Rosie hurried into a doorway, drawing well back, waiting till the second bus was gone. Then she stepped down onto the path and looked around her. The morning was bright and crisp, the street quiet, no longer ringing with shouts and laughter. Her watch set, mind focussed on her own time Rosie closed her eyes until the surrounding hush gave way to a mighty roar of traffic.

From the window of the sick bay, Stacia Bolger watched. Her eyes widened and she gasped with disbelief as the girl vanished into the atmosphere.

Chapter 30

Rosie stood blinking in the winter sunlight, dressed again for the 21st century. The Cork train was due in at three o'clock and Mum and Dad weren't expecting her yet. She had time to kill. Thinking of Jennie, unhappiness welled. She would miss her and Katie and Jimmy . . . and even Old Misery. Her thoughts were full of them and it wasn't yet time to move on. Aimlessly she wandered down the street and into town. Every inch of O'Connell Street was filled with decorations and Christmas songs blared from the shops. Putting her hands into her pockets to keep them warm, she found the butterfly brooch. The only memento of her journey, she clasped it tightly.

There was only one place she could go, Rosie decided, before she switched fully into the 21st century.

Twenty minutes later she was standing in front of Jennie's picture in the National Gallery, looking with nostalgia at the houses and the streetlamps and the quiet street. Even the white boots caused a pang of loss. She studied the painting for a long time, conscious after a while that someone was standing behind her. Not wanting to be disturbed Rosie didn't turn around, willing the other person to go away.

"So, what do you think?" The voice was American, female.

"Yeah, fine, whatever." Rudeness might get rid of the woman.

The American didn't move and Rosie sighed, no longer able to concentrate. She turned to go.

"Hi, Rosie," the woman smiled, older, much older, but after a few moments, still Jennie. Her eyes and smile were the same and Rosie stared, transfixed.

"I got into town last week. Patrick is back at the hotel. We're staying at The Shelbourne."

Looking at the elegant woman with the short dark hair, Rosie tried to take in the transformation. In one way it was only a couple of hours since she'd seen her and the change was extraordinary.

Jennie seized her arm. "Let's go for a coffee. Then you can catch up on my life if you like."

That Christmas in 1963, Jennie had gone to New York and had never come back to St Catherine's. Her father had decided he needed to look after the American side of his business and so the move became permanent and because her parents missed her too much, Jennie stayed on. Eventually Patrick closed the Irish branch of the company and the house in Dublin was sold.

After High School Jennie studied Art, then went to Paris where she'd met her husband, Michel de Beauvoir. Paris was where she lived and painted, where her children

Louise and Bertrand worked. Next week they were coming over with Michel for Christmas.

"I came to the gallery today because someone in the hotel mentioned the exhibition and I saw you. It was a shock seeing you. More than half my life is over, yet you're still the same."

They didn't speak for a while, thinking about time. Then Jennie said, "By the way, Patrick rang your parents and explained the family connection. Don't worry, he didn't mention you. Your gran spoke to him and we're invited to the party."

Catching a movement nearby Rosie looked up and saw a woman staring at their table.

"Excuse me," the woman said, coming over. "I wonder if by any chance you're Jennie O'Neill?" When Jennie nodded she continued, "I'm so pleased to meet you again. I wrote the short introduction about you in the catalogue of school prize-winners."

Rosie thought the face was familiar but couldn't place her.

"We used to be at school together," the woman went on. "I'm Stacey Sheldon – Sheldon is my married name. You'd have known me as Stacia Bolger."

Rosie's mouth opened and she said without thinking, "You wrote the blurb – no wonder it's wrong! Jennie was never expelled."

Taken aback, Stacia said, "I don't know who you are, dear, but my facts are right as far as I know them. Jennie left school one Christmas without explanation. Word went around that she'd been expelled."

"It's a lie!" Rosie was indignant.

"I wasn't to know that. She disappeared, was never heard of again. It seemed to me she was in some sort of disgrace." Triumphantly she added, turning to Jennie, "And you never produced one piece of worthwhile art again."

Jennie smiled, "I've been painting a lot under my married name: Jeanne de Beauvoir."

Stacia paled and from her intake of breath, Rosie realised she recognised the name and that Jennie must be well known in the Art world.

"What are you doing, Stacia? Are you painting?"

"It's Stacey." She shook her head, "No, I'm not. I studied Architecture. I've found it less pretentious and more enriching than Art. Now I run my own practice. Look, I'm sorry my facts were wrong. "

"They're not facts!" Rosie was still indignant, not liking the woman at all.

"Not to worry," Jennie said. "It doesn't matter."

The women chatted for a while about St Catherine's and Stacia said Delia Waters was doing very well for herself. She had married a fellow from Ivor's, a Jimmy Sullivan. "Their travel company must be worth a fortune," Stacia said, adding, "and you know she was my best friend in school."

Jennie had more news. She'd looked up Katie MacAllister since coming back and she was now principal of a large community school in Cork, information that amazed Rosie, since Katie hadn't exactly been a model student. She thought of Jimmy. A travel company seemed exactly right for him.

Conversation between the two women petered out and, looking at her watch, Stacia said she must fly. When she was gone, Jennie smiled, "Life hasn't turned out too badly, has it? Time has been kind."

Rosie considered. Time made people age and die, but this last journey into the past had brought Jennie into her life and soon she would meet Patrick again. They and their family would be part of her future.

Yes, Time had been kind.

The End

Direct to your home!

If you enjoyed this book why not
visit our website:

www.poolbeg.com

and get another book delivered straight to
your home or to a friend's home!

www.poolbeg.com

All orders are despatched within 24 hours.

Also by poolbeg.com

Rosie's Century

ANN CARROLL

A letter from the past, a set of clues, the threat of murder – these bring Rosie back to the gas-lit streets of Dublin 1900 for another great adventure.

It is April and Queen Victoria is about to visit the city. Rosie has learnt nothing in school about this event and she's amazed at the Dubliners' enthusiasm for the queen. But beneath the holiday atmosphere evil lurks . . .

ISBN 978-1-85371-972-1

Also by poolbeg.com

Rosie's War

ANN CARROLL

Time-traveller Rosie finds an old newspaper, dated 19th July 1943, and spots a report on the arrest of one Edward O'Neill for murder. Rosie is horrified: this is the Edward she met on her trip to 1900, son of her Great-Great-Uncle Joseph!

Remembering the brave, fun-loving boy, Rosie has no choice: she must time-travel to 1943 in the hope of helping him.

She takes her rollerblades - and a few snacks like popcorn and chocolate. She might have packed differently if she had known that food was rationed in Dublin in 1943! Ireland is in a state of 'Emergency' as the Second World War rages in Britain and Europe . . .

But Rosie has survived harsh conditions before. The important thing is: can she save Edward?

ISBN 978-1-84223-073-2

Also by poolbeg.com

Rosie's Quest

Ann Carroll

Dublin, Friday the 13th January 1956:
A playground accident affects the lives of twin girls forever.
After all, there is no way to alter the past . . . or is there?

Rosie McGrath travels back in time to 1956.
Can she survive in that harsher world?
Will she be trapped there?
Can she change the events of that long-ago Friday
when her mother and aunt went their separate ways?

ISBN 978-1-85371-281-4